PRISONERS OF WAR

THE PATH
TO HEAVEN

BRIAN CRAWFORD

EPIC
Press

The Path to Heaven
Prisoners of War: Book #6

Written by Brian Crawford

Copyright © 2017 by Abdo Consulting Group, Inc.

Published by EPIC Press™
PO Box 398166
Minneapolis, MN 55439

Cover design by Christina Doffing
Images for cover art obtained from iStockPhoto.com
Edited by Gil Conrad

LIBRARY OF CONGRESS CATALOGING-IN-PUBLICATION DATA

Names: Crawford, Brian, author.
Title: Path to heaven / by Brian Crawford.
Description: Minneapolis, MN : EPIC Press, [2017] | Series: Prisoners of war ; book #6
Summary: Himmelweg burns, grenades explode, and machine guns fire as Julia, Eric, Józef, and
   Russ escape. While Julia and Eric are hidden and then denounced by a Polish priest, Russ
   and Eric join the Red Army to fight the Nazis.
Identifiers: LCCN 2016931782 | ISBN 9781680763560 (lib. bdg.) |
   ISBN 9781680763423 (ebook)
Subjects: LCSH: Prisoners—Fiction. | Prisoner-of-war camps—Fiction. | Escaped prisoners—
   Fiction. | Interpersonal relationships—Fiction. | Survival—Fiction. | Human behavior—
   Fiction. | Young adult fiction.
Classification: DDC [Fic]—dc23
LC record available at http://lccn.loc.gov/2016931782

EPIC
Press

EPICPRESS.COM

T 24678

Dedicated to all those who resist persecution and tyranny, in whatever form.

"Hell is empty and all the devils are here."
—William Shakespeare

Certain events in this novel were inspired by actual prisoner revolts from death camps and POW camps during the Second World War. All characters are fictional.

ОДИН
ONE

L IKE THE DETONATION OF A STARTER PISTOL, AN electrical popping sound triggered the prisoner revolt in Himmelweg.

The nearly five hundred prisoners stood at attention in the *Appellplatz*, where they'd been assembled for morning roll call just a half hour before. But nine were missing—the eight who'd positioned themselves around the camp with rifles and bayonets, and Éric, who'd just succeeded in shorting the camp's transformer and cutting the electricity from the barbed wire surrounding the death camp.

"This is it!" Józef hissed from his place in his column. His words snapped Julia out of her daze.

She turned to look at him, her eyes glazed and watery. Józef had just told her that the revolt was underway, and her head reeled with the realization that she could soon be dead. Her face ashen, she nodded as if to say, *What the hell do we do?*

Around the hundreds of assembled prisoners, the German and Ukrainian guards flitted about in a panic. Just minutes before the transformer blew, the S.S. had begun to realize that their roll call numbers fell short. Prisoners were unaccounted for, and this had never happened in the history of Himmelweg. Under the gallows, Commandant Strauss stood transfixed, his Luger pistol in his right hand and his black leather whip in his left. Alerted by the explosion, he stood with his legs shoulder-width apart and arms out to his sides, as if ready to fight the first person who even so much as glanced at him.

But he wasn't looking at the prisoners. His eyes were leveled above their heads, and the prisoners' snakelike black pupils darted to the barracks, to the sorting shed, and back toward the officers' quarters, where tendrils of black smoke bled into the morning sky. As Strauss watched in horror, the smoke was thickening.

Back behind Strauss, three guards sprinted, their boots and gear clanking and clinking, toward the officers' quarters, where the camp's main electric transformer lay, and where Éric had headed two hours before to short out the camp's power.

Strauss saw that chaos and panic were infecting all the guards. Although he couldn't hear them, in the towers around the camp's perimeter, the guards spat German obscenities back and forth as they leaned over the edge of the towers' crow's nests to peer at the burning buildings and the barbed wire fence, which no longer buzzed with its usual ten thousand volts.

Back among the now wavering lines of prisoners, Józef darted his eyes around at the smoke and unnerved Germans. He turned his head toward Julia. This was an act which—if seen—would earn him a beating, or worse. But because the camp guards were distracted by the growing chaos around them, this act of defiance went unnoticed.

"He's done it! Éric's cut the power. And they've set fire to the buildings. Now when we hear—"

BAM! BAM! BAMBAMBAM!

Józef couldn't finish his sentence before volleys of rifle fire erupted from around the *Appellplatz*, sending every German and Ukrainian guard ducking and whipping out his rifle or pistol. Like crippled turtles trying in vain to pull their heads into their shells, the guards whirled around wildly, looking for the source of the gunfire. Józef and Julia also turned to look, as did many of the assembled prisoners, but, unlike the others, Józef and Julia knew where to look.

BAM! BAMBAM!

Lightning-quick puffs of blue-white smoke erupted from underneath the sorting shed, the barracks, and the officers' quarters. The hidden members of the informal escape committee, who had slipped out into the predawn dark hours with their stolen rifles and ammunition, were now using their precious bullets to target the guards and machine gunners in the watchtowers. The bullets belched forth from underneath the buildings, and the silhouettes of the watchtower guards slumped away, leaving the emptiness of the wooden crow's nests hunched against the red morning light. The bullets were finding their marks.

"Now!" Without looking at her, Józef swung his right hand and yanked Julia's arm so hard that her head snapped back as her body lurched forward. He kept his eyes glued on Strauss and the other guards, who had just begun to sprint toward the source of the resistance gunfire, leaving the prisoners standing confused in the *Appellplatz*.

This was their cue to move.

Like an ocean being stirred by the winds of a violent storm, the undulating, shorn heads of the assembled prisoners stirred and ebbed. Some dared to turn their heads in the confusion; others bent their heads forward in prayer. A few disappeared as prisoners dropped to their knees. Among these, a group of fifty or so pushed their way from the ranks, shoving others aside as they ran, screaming.

"This is it! The wires are down! We're killing the guards! RUN!"

These were the fifty or so prisoners that had been in Barrack 13 when Russ, Józef, Julia, and Éric had planned the revolt, and when the six rifles Antonín stole after the bombing were divvied out. Their plan had been to use the rifles and fires to create just enough confusion that would allow the others to storm through the front gate, which was now no longer electrified. But where was Éric now? And Russ? He'd gone out that morning with a rifle and some bullets, but neither Józef nor Julia knew where he'd gone, nor where he might be hiding.

So far, the plan was working. The guards were falling. The wire was down.

It was time to run.

"Go! Run! Don't you see! It's now or never!" The prisoners of Barrack 13 continued to push through the rows gathered in the *Appellplatz* and made their way southward, toward the camp's main gates. A few of the prisoners they pushed woke from their stupor and followed. Others resisted and stayed put, too terrified to move, even though doing so would mean their death in the S.S. reprisals that would certainly come.

BAMBAMBAMBAM! BAMBAM!

The camp erupted into ear-splitting, bone-rattling gunfire as the S.S. and the Ukrainian guards on the ground opened fire at the source of the gunshots: the buildings' crawlspaces. Several of the farther watchtowers burst into screaming volleys of orange machine-gun fire, but the distance between them and the *Appellplatz* made it difficult for any of the bullets to reach the prisoners. Still, massive divots and piles of red earth burst from the frozen ground as the bullets rained down. As for the towers nearest the prisoners, they now contained only corpses.

Around the perimeter of the *Appellplatz*, flames

engulfed the sorting shed, two barracks, and the officers' quarters. The prisoners sent out that morning to start the fires had been successful. What had begun as tendrils of black smoke now bulged and surged into billows of flame and acrid smoke. Windows glowed orange and white as the flames licked the buildings' façades and awnings. Glass shattered from the heat. Wood splintered, popped, and sizzled.

As the gunfire, shouts, and flames swelled to an inferno, Józef and Julia broke from their ranks and joined the seventy or so prisoners that were now funneling frenetically through the others and towards the front gate. Together, they formed one solid line of movement, like a massive snake pushing its way through the viscous mud of some putrid swamp.

Closer, closer, closer . . . *"Die Häftlinge sind auf der Flucht!"* screamed one of the guards somewhere off to Józef's left, near the sorting shed. *The prisoners are fleeing!* Józef jerked his head in the guard's direction, only to see him crumple to the ground as a gunshot echoed from behind him. As the guard fell, Józef glimpsed a form moving about in the mud underneath the sorting shed. The grayish, prone form of a prisoner. A prisoner with a rifle.

It was Russ.

Looking over the sights of his weapon, Russ allowed a brief smile to cross his face as his eyes met Józef's. Russ winked. In that instant, the two seemed to say to each other, almost telepathically, *It'll be alright. We can do this.* But no sooner had Józef made eye contact with the American than he again pulled Julia along with him and toward the front gate, where a dozen or so prisoners were already pushing with all their weight against the latch. Creaking, the gate bulged and strained in resistance.

In the years since he'd arrived in the camp, Józef had seen at least six prisoners meet their death against the wire, either because they'd tried to escape, or because an enraged guard had hurled a prisoner into the electrified fence. Each time, the prisoner's body had snapped, popped, and writhed under the weight of ten thousand volts. Each time, the smell of burning flesh had lingered over the camp as the Germans left the body there to roast as a reminder and warning to others. Now, seeing the prisoners grabbing at the wire with impunity, Józef couldn't help but stifle a gut reaction of terror.

During this time, the Germans hadn't been blind, deaf, or dumb. Even though they'd been distracted by the snipers, the fires, and the power failure in the fence, they quickly circled around the swarming prisoners and opened fire with their sub-machine guns and with their pistols. When they ran out of bullets, they slashed out with their whips.

On either side of the column of rushing prison-ers, men and women dropped to the ground, their bloodied bodies riddled with bullets. When Józef saw what was happening, he pulled Julia toward the middle of the crowd, hoping that they would be safer that way. But no sooner had he rushed to the middle than a pang of soul-wrenching guilt filled him. He was using his comrades as human shields. Why was he not helping his brothers and sisters? What kind of a monster had this camp reduced him to?

Still, he had little time for remorse. For no sooner had the Germans and Ukrainians opened fire on the prisoners—some at near point-blank range—than the snipers under the buildings adjusted their aim from the watchtowers to the guards on foot. Because of the ear-splitting gunfire, Józef would not have known that the snipers were fighting back had he not seen the guards falling in agony, their faces contorted from the shock of having been shot from behind. The roar of gunfire was deafening.

But the prisoners' window was opening wider.

With a wrenching crack, KL Himmelweg's front gates finally gave way against the weight of the nearly hundred men and women pushing against it. When they swung open, the prisoners up front were tossed to the ground as nothing more pushed back against them. Behind them, a stampede ensued, with the other panicked prisoners jostling and shoving for a place up front, out of the gates and away from the camp. As people began to pour from the gates and trample down the dirt road with what little strength they had left, the guards back in the camp hopped from building to building as they tried to avoid the sniper fire. The guards then shot at the backs of those running away from the camp and across the road and field to the thick forest beyond.

By this time, Józef had already dragged Julia with him through the gates, over the bodies littering the ground, and away, away, away. Though she tried to keep up, she cried out in agony as Józef pounded forward. Józef knew that her already weakened body could not take much more of this pounding and jostling. Sweat covered both of their faces, but Julia's face had a yellowish, ashen hue. How much longer would she last?

Somewhere behind them, there was a lull in

the gunfire. What was happening? Why had the Germans stopped shooting? Remembering that each of the committee snipers had taken only ten bullets, Józef wondered if they were out of ammunition yet. If so, then what? How would they get out?

And Éric?

And Russ?

The forest rushed up to greet them. On either side of Józef, prisoners thrust their way into the cover and immediately scattered, running, running, running in all directions. Still clutching Julia by the arm, Józef pushed through the brambles, bushes, and briars, listening to the sound of his wooden clogs crushing the frozen, dead leaves and detritus at his feet. It was a sound he hadn't heard in years, for his ears had grown accustomed to the ugly wooden scrape-clump of his clogs against mud, against rock, and against wood. But not against the softness of the forest floor.

"Wait, stop. I can't . . . " Julia pulled against Józef's hand, her body becoming heavier and heavier as she slipped toward the ground. At first Józef yanked back stubbornly, but then he stopped and turned.

At his feet, Julia had collapsed into a pile. She was clutching her right side with her fist, and her face was twisted in pain. A bright red splotch of blood soaked her prisoner's uniform from the crotch and down both legs.

"Are you hit?" he asked, his eyes shifting from Julia back to the camp, which was now striated by the lines of elm and poplar trees that had pushed up between them. Massive billows of smoke saturated the morning sky as the camp's buildings burned. Though they were now nearly one hundred meters away, Józef could see that none of the Germans or Ukrainians had followed the prisoners into the forest. And then he realized why. Three to four hundred prisoners were still in the camp. Between them and the fires, the guards probably had turned their attention to securing the camp, rather than risking lives chasing several dozen prisoners into the forest. *Why didn't the others run? Try to escape like us?* Józef tried to peer through the trees and fence to see what other prisoners might be left standing in the *Appellplatz. Don't they know the Germans will not let this escape go unpunished? Don't they know that staying behind is suicide?* He shook his head and spat before kneeling before Julia. He placed his hand on her forehead. It was searing and damp. Julia's lips were trembling and her arms and legs were shaking.

"No, I'm not hit," she replied, her fading voice shaking as much as the rest of her body. "It's my side. My kidney. I'm pissing blood. And I can't stop. Where I was shot before. Before the camp. I . . . " Her face twisted in agony, and she clenched her eyes shut. Tears streamed down both cheeks. "I . . . "

Józef didn't let her finish. Glancing up one last time at the camp, he reached over with his right hand and latched it around her wrist. With one heave and a grunt, he hoisted her to a sitting position. Her head lolled to the side and her eyes rolled back into her head, revealing jaundiced whites. Józef grunted once more and pulled his friend up and onto his back. Her stomach now lay across his shoulders in a fireman's carry. With his left hand, he held her wrist and he snaked his right arm between her legs to steady her.

Despite the years of penury, malnutrition, and sickness, he stood, turned his back to the camp, and pushed his way into the forest.

ДВА
TWO

"JÓZEF!"

Someone called out from the thickness of the trees and bushes.

Józef froze. His legs, arms, and shoulders burning from carrying Julia, he turned toward the voice.

"Who is it?" he hissed into the undergrowth. By now he had managed to put about a mile between himself and the camp. Still, he shuddered in terror at the sound of his own voice. Besides his footsteps and his and Julia's breathing, it was the only noise out there. All of the other prisoners had by now vanished to different corners of the forest.

"What?" he hissed again, rotating his upper body so that he could see behind and around him.

A crunch.

A snap.

Footsteps.

Someone was pushing through the forest. Heading in their direction. It couldn't be a German—Józef thought he'd recognized the voice. Could it be . . . ?

"Józef! It's me!" With these words, a figure emerged from behind a clump of young trees. It was Russ.

Almost smiling but covered in sweat and mud, the American pushed his way over the leaves to Józef and Julia, who groaned weakly. In his left hand, Russ clutched the stolen rifle. As he bounded over to the two Poles, he held his right arm out for balance. A wave of relief flooded over Józef.

"It's you!" he said, his shoulders relaxing. "How did you get out?"

"Ha! Krauts were so busy with the fires and the

others that I slipped out and got through another part of the fence, where they weren't looking. I don't think they even saw me, the idiots."

"The rifle? Do you have any bullets left?"

Russ took the weapon into both hands, looked down, and eased the receiver back two inches. He let it snap closed and removed the magazine, which was empty. Replacing the magazine, he looked up at Józef.

"One bullet left. In the chamber. Better make it count."

"And the other shots?"

"Nine bullets. Nine dead Germans."

"In the towers?"

"Some, yes. But when all hell broke lose and those bastards on the ground started shooting, I capped off some of them, too."

"My God."

Russ took a deep breath and wiped his glistening forehead with the back of his right sleeve. Józef saw that the American's hand was trembling.

"I was supposed to be going home before all this shit happened," Russ said, his voice wavering. "I'm a pilot, for Chrissakes. Not a goddamned sniper."

He sighed and looked Józef in the eye.

"We have to go. They'll be comin'." He paused, looking at Julia. "How is she? Hit?"

"No, she—" Józef began, but Julia lifted her head and spoke.

"No. Put me down."

Józef glanced over his shoulder at her. He then looked at the American with a puzzled expression, seeking advice on what to do. Russ nodded and closed his eyes, as if to say, *Go ahead. Do what she says.*

Józef squatted and leaned to his right, letting Julia's dangling feet rest on the leaves. Russ laid his rifle down and stepped forward, cradling her head in his hands and supporting her back as Józef rolled her down and onto her back. She relaxed into the leaves. Russ noticed that the front of her pants was soaked in blood. As if someone had tossed a cup of red paint onto her abdomen. Julia laid her head back into the leaves. She was breathing heavily, her chest heaving up and down.

"I need to walk on my own," she said, easing her elbows up to support her upper body. Her skin was pale and clammy. Had she not been moving, she would've looked like a corpse herself.

Russ fidgeted in place, nervous. As he spoke, he constantly jerked his head around to look in all directions. Like a rabbit on the lookout for a hawk.

"Can you?" he asked, wringing his hands together. He leaned over and picked his rifle up, looking back at Józef. He stood. "Józef and I can take turns carryin' you . . . "

"No!" Julia snapped, pulling herself to her feet. As she stood, she inched her way over to a tree and placed her hand on the rough bark, supporting her wavering body. "I can do this."

With that, she took a step forward. Paused. Filled her lungs with air. Grabbed her side. And took another step.

Józef and Russ walked on either side of her as she staggered forward. Not wanting to fully reveal their concern to Julia, they held their arms to their sides as if walking normally. But they kept their gaze locked on her tottering gait and their arms, ready to spring out to catch her should she fall.

Step. Step. Step.

With each step, Julia seemed to gain in strength and confidence. Like a toddler leaving its mother's arms for the first time. The color was still absent from her face, but her eyes shone with a fierce determination that Józef had not seen in some time. Julia clenched her jaw and stepped, stepped, stepped, gaining momentum as she put first one, then ten, then thirty more meters between her and the camp.

"Are you still bleedin'?" Russ asked after two minutes. He glanced at Julia's blood-soaked pants, which glistened in the midmorning light. Julia looked down but kept walking. She shook her head.

"I don't think so," she said. "I don't feel anything running anymore. It must've been the stress and bouncing around back there to try and get out."

Russ looked over at Józef.

"Look," he said, stepping up to Julia's side, "you've got to let us support some of your weight. You can still walk. But we'll go faster that way. And now we *have* to go faster."

Russ slid his right arm under Julia's left and behind her back. The warmth of her body crept in through his uniform and warmed his arm. She said nothing, but reached over and clutched his shoulders, leaning her weight into him. On her right, Józef did the same. Without talking, both men lifted gently and quickened their pace. The six-legged escapee now shuffled stealthily through the forest, over hills, around brambles, through bushes, behind trees. As Russ and Józef walked, Julia's legs moved in time with theirs, though her feet hardly touched the ground. Her gait was more like a dance step with just two steps: left, right, left, right, left, right, left. As they moved, she bit her lip against the pain, which now crept up from her kidney and into her back and shoulders. Her entire body had begun to scream under the support of the two men. Left, right, left, right, left, right.

SCREEEEEEEEECH!

From behind them somewhere, a whistle pierced the forest. Shouts immediately followed. Shouts in German.

They were coming.

Russ halted and jerked his head around to look behind him. Nothing. Just forest.

"Move it!" he snapped, quickening his pace to a slight jog. Józef also sped up, and Julia tried to keep pace, but every other step her feet slid over the leaves and detritus as the two men pulled her along. Panicked, they shuffled through the forest. It was difficult to tell if the sounds behind them were the sounds of the Germans approaching, or if it was just the echo of their own crippled footsteps off the snarling trees.

Faster and faster they rushed, tripping, dragging, scraping. Julia's face contorted in agony, while Russ's and Józef's arms and legs seared from the effort, fatigue, and terror.

Shouts from behind.

Another whistle.

Were the Germans shouting at *them*? Had the Germans seen them? Or were they shouting at someone else? If so, who? What other prisoners? How many had actually made it out? Since they fled they hadn't turned back to see. Was Éric with any of them? Was he by himself?

"Aaaahhh, I can't do this!" Julia seethed, trying to pull herself up with her arms and put weight on her legs. Each time she did, her knees failed her and she lurched forward, causing Russ and Józef to lose their balance—if ever so slightly, but still enough to cause the three to slow. Faces red and sweaty from exertion, the two men surged forward, driven by adrenaline and fear.

"Leave me!" Julia said, shaking her head and

allowing her arms to go limp. "I'm just going to get you two killed. Do it!"

Shaking their heads in unison, Russ and Józef held firm, pulling her back up so that her head was level with theirs.

"No!" Józef said, speaking to Julia in Polish. "You're one of us! We can't . . . ahhhhhhh!"

Before he could finish his sentence, the three pitched as a whole over the edge of an embankment hidden behind a patch of blackthorn. The ground had disappeared from under their feet. Russ's and Józef's arms flew from Julia's shoulders, and each held their arms out, now trying to prevent themselves from slamming into a tree, log, or root. Their backs, their legs, their chests, their arms, their hands—their entire bodies were hurled left and right, up and down. They rolled and slid and thumped and crashed to a stop seven meters below. The drop had not been straight down, but the angle of the embankment was steep enough to give them—if only for an instant—the feeling of free-falling. With a thud and a bone-twisting crunch, they slid to a stop, Julia and Russ on their backs and Józef in pushup position on his face.

"You okay?" Julia asked, pushing herself into a sitting position. The two men rolled over and sat up, brushing themselves off.

"Yes," Józef answered, looking up to the top of the embankment. "Damn cliff."

"Where's the gun?" Russ said, standing. He jerked his head around, his eyes scanning the leaves and sticks.

"Over there," Julia said, pointing off to her left. The rifle had landed two meters away from the three, its muzzle pointing uphill. Russ hopped over Julia's legs and picked up the weapon. He turned it over in his hand and looked sideways into the barrel to make sure no mud or dirt had clogged it.

BAM! BAMBAM!

From up above, distant gunshots rang out. Far-off shouts mingled in with the report, echoing off the otherwise quiet Polish forest and countryside beyond.

"Shit! They're still on the move!" Józef said, jumping to his feet. He stepped over and held his hand out to Julia, who took it. He pulled her to a standing position and placed his arm around her back. She swatted it away and looked around. A little color had returned to her face. "Look! Down there!" She pointed behind Józef and down the hill, which formed a gentle slope from where they were. Józef and Russ turned around.

About two hundred meters away, the pale gray of a winding, paved road oozed through the thinning trees, which almost looked like a series of prison bars holding them inside the world of the camp, while the free world—the civilized world—jeered at them from beyond.

"I wonder where it goes?" Russ wondered aloud. "And where we even are?"

"I *know* where we are," Julia answered. "My village is only nine or ten kilometers away from here."

"How can you possibly know that?" Russ snapped. Józef too looked at Julia in disbelief.

"When I was back on our farm, I heard screams from the transports and came to see for myself. That's how I was caught. Trying to help the people on the trains." She paused and took a deep breath, avoiding their eyes. "And that's how my brother was shot."

More commotion from above, back in the forest.

Józef looked back up the hill and then toward the road. His eyes bulged with terror.

"Well, we can't go down there now, hm, not in the middle of the day!" he snapped. He reached down and grabbed the sides of his prisoner's shirt, the filthy white-and-gray striped uniform that he'd worn for the past three years. On the shirt's left breast, a yellow inverted triangle was clumsily stitched underneath the broad identification number stenciled in black: SB87433. He ran his hand over his shaved head.

"And look at us!" he pointed to the other two. "And you!" this time, to Julia. "If we go down there and someone sees us, they'd know who we are right away! And you're covered in blood. Even if we had civilian clothes, they'd be able to tell who we were just by looking at our heads, hm, and we weigh twenty kilos less than anyone on the outside."

Russ looked around at the embankment and surrounding trees. He clutched the rifle with his right hand. Julia bent over and rubbed at the bloodstain covering the inside of her pants. It almost seemed as if by doing so, she was just trying to make a point to Józef, because no amount of rubbing would be able to get the blood out. There was just too much.

"Over there!" Russ snapped, causing Julia to jump. Without waiting for the other two to respond, he strode with wide steps off to Józef's right and along the embankment, heading towards a thick clump of brambles and briars that clung to a more rocky portion of the ridge like a massive blob trying to creep its way up the hill. As he covered the ten or fifteen meters to the spot, several more gunshots echoed through the countryside. In the distance, another whistle pierced the air.

When he reached the bush, Russ planted his foot directly in the middle of the plant and thrust his rifle in, muzzle first. With both hands, he gripped the weapon's wooden stock and pulled to the side, lifting one flank of the bramble up and over. This revealed a dark opening between two coffin-sized rocks and disappearing into the embankment—a hole about three-by-four feet in size. One big enough to admit a person. Russ leaned over and peered into the darkness.

"It's a cave," he said stepping in and looking deeper. "We should all fit."

"What? Stay here?" Józef said. "They'll be on us in no time!"

Julia's eyes lingered on the road, but she turned to Józef.

"What choice do we have?" she snapped. "None

of us saw it because of the bushes. It's either hide there and hope the Germans don't come poking about, or go down to the road in daylight and be caught by the first patrol. And God knows with an escape, there will be patrols. And who knows how many?"

Józef hesitated, his eyes shifting between the cave, the road, and the forest above. The sound of a far-off crash and crack, followed by several men's voices, made him hop back to Julia and Russ.

"All right, hm, let's go!" he snapped, hopping over to where Russ stood. He passed Julia, grabbing her by the left arm. She shook him off as he repeated, "Come on!"

Behind him, Julia clenched her jaw and shook her head. She hurried after him. Her legs still quivered, but she held her arms out and quickly covered the distance to the cave. When she reached the opening, Józef had already disappeared inside. Russ held out the briars, which formed a sort of natural, camouflaged doorway. Once she had pushed her way into the dark and settled on an angular outcropping of freezing stones, Russ backed his way in and let the bush fall closed, blocking out most of the light.

In the cave, which was no bigger than a small closet, the sound of shivering, wheezing breaths echoed off the stone walls, giving the three of them the impression that they were inside a quivering, panting machine. Without speaking, Julia and Józef slid up against each other, noiselessly allowing their bodies to touch and exchange what little heat they had left. In front of them, Russ crouched with his back to them. The butt of the rifle protruded slightly from behind the American as he kept the muzzle pointed towards the cave entrance. He took a deep, audible breath, and turned his head slightly over his right shoulder. In the gloom, he couldn't see Józef and Julia, but he felt their meager warmth and frantic wisps of breath.

"I've got one shot left," he whispered. "All we can hope for is if they come, they'll think we have a lot more and maybe we can kill one in the bargain. No noise! All we have now is hope."

Somewhere in the distance, a gunshot echoed. Two. Five. Julia snapped her head toward the cave's entrance.

"The others," she whispered, her lower lip trembling from the cold. Russ followed her gaze out of their hideout. He took a deep breath, his chest visibly swelling, before letting it out again with a *whoosh*.

"Yeah," he said. "The others. We can't do anythin' for them now. It's everyone for 'emselves. All we can hope for is that the Krauts will follow 'em all over creation so fewer soldiers chase after us."

"What if we see someone else? Another prisoner?" Józef asked, his eyes wide on the American. "Should we stick together?"

Russ frowned and shook his head. "No," he said. "Too much risk. A small group moves faster than a big one. We'll just keep our fingers crossed that they can get out. Get away. But"—he lifted the rifle and gripped it with both hands, as if preparing for a gunfight—"they're on their own. Just like us."

THREE

NIGHT.

Julia stirred. Sitting up in the dark, she threw her hands out to her sides. Where was she? Her back screamed in agony, and her legs had gone numb. They felt like great masses of flesh attached to her body, which shivered uncontrollably. Her teeth clattered, sending a hollow, rattling echo back into her ears.

Then she remembered: The escape. The running. The blood. The hiding. And now here she was, cramped in a tiny cave with Józef and Russ.

She sat up and noticed that her head no longer spun as it had been doing for the past day. She blinked and rubbed her eyes. White and black dots no longer polluted her vision. Under her back, Józef's immobile legs formed a sort of improvised, bony mattress. His breaths came slow and heavy. And Russ? Before she had lost consciousness from the sheer fatigue and emotional exhaustion from the escape, his silhouette had been the last thing she saw. Framed by the irregular shape of the cave's mouth, Russ had become a statue. Hunched over his stolen rifle, he had trained the weapon's muzzle on the jagged, crisscrossed tangle of briars and brambles covering the entrance, ready should anyone try to enter. That was at least ten hours ago. And now? Russ had collapsed backwards onto Julia's legs, cutting off their circulation. The steady rhythm of his breathing indicated that he too had succumbed from the exhaustion and strain of everything they'd suffered—over the past years and the past twenty-four hours.

Sitting up, Julia rubbed her hands together, trying to bring warmth to her rigid and cramped fingers. She worked life back into her hands. And as she did, a paroxysm of pain shot from her kidney and through her entire body. She grimaced. Breathing slowly and evenly, she squeezed her eyes shut until the pain passed. She took a deep breath, filling her lungs to bursting and waking herself up. She took another. In the dark, she tried to make out Russ's and Józef's forms in front of and behind her. Nothing—they were just amorphous masses of suffering, trying desperately to survive but succumbing to sleep, the sister of Death.

Death—who would no doubt find them much faster if Julia stayed with them. She couldn't run. She couldn't keep up. Her body was failing her. And now she couldn't fail *them*.

She had to leave.

Moving bit by bit, she placed her hands on the stone cave walls and pushed herself slowly up. As she moved, shards of fire and ice rocketed through her sleeping legs. After moving several centimeters, she waited for the feeling to return to her legs and the pain to subside. When it had abated, she inched up farther, farther, farther, carefully working her legs from out from under Russ's slumbering frame. At one point she slipped, causing his shoulder to fall back and hit the stone ground, but all Russ did was to snort and continue sleeping. For a moment, Julia had the impression that she could simply yank her legs from under him and he wouldn't budge.

With her legs free, Julia worked her feet nimbly over Russ's body. Keeping her hands anchored on the cave walls, she lifted her legs high and placed her feet on either side of the sleeping American, step by step. Even though she felt his body pushing against her wooden clogs as she moved, Russ never stirred.

And then, with one push of her left hand, she thrust the briars from over the cave's mouth and stepped into the night air.

Taking a deep breath, she realized that their body heat had warmed the cave considerably. The frigid Polish night lanced her with tongues of rime and frost. She took a step away from the cave and turned around. In the crescent moonlight, she could just discern the mass of bushes covering the cave's entrance. She leaned to the left. To the right. Looking at the bushes from several angles. It seemed camouflaged.

Satisfied, she turned toward the road and worked her way down the gentle incline. Step after brittle step, she clutched her body with her shaking and atrophied arms in a feeble attempt to keep herself warm. But the effort was mostly mental. Tremors tore at her entire body. And Julia knew that without help, she would be dead in a few hours.

When she was within five meters of the road, she stopped. Above, the Polish night sky shone clear with the thin light of the moon offset by a million stars. In other circumstances, she may have lain down in warm clothing to gaze at the beautiful night sky, lost in the beauty of the constellations, the shooting stars, the Milky Way. But now she crouched down for another reason: to remain hidden from passing cars, whose white headlights pierced the darkness with an eye-straining violence that stung her retinas.

She didn't have to wait long. From far off to the right, the hissing buzz of a motor broke the night's stillness. Louder and louder it became, coming this way. She pulled her entire body and head into a stinging clump of overgrowth lining an ill-cut drainage ditch at the side of the road. Above all, she made sure to pull her shoulders out of sight for fear that the grayness of her striped uniform would be more visible than her skeletal face and head.

Headlights. Low to the ground. Whoever it was, they were in a car. One of the low-riding kinds driven by German officers. A Mercedes.

Another vehicle approached. A truck. A military truck close on the tail of the car. Its engine roaring as it pulled its weight up the gentle incline and rumbled by. Once it passed, Julia peered from her hideout at the vehicle. In the dark, she couldn't make out the drivers, but she could see that the rear of the truck was covered by a green cloth canopy that jostled with the vehicle's movements and the wind blowing from the front.

Germans. No doubt scouring the countryside for any escaped prisoners, who—she glanced down at her blood-crusted and rime-covered uniform—shouldn't be too hard to find.

When the vehicles had moved by, their glowing red taillights fading into the dark, Julia let out a long sigh. Only then did she realize she'd been holding her breath. She kept her eyes riveted on the curve in the road around which they'd disappeared, as if expecting them to halt, do a U-turn, and circle back to swoop in on her. But they didn't. Once the sound of their engines had completely faded, the only sound that remained was the silence of the winter night, Julia's frenetic breath, and the incessant rattling of her teeth and skull. The previous sounds of the pursuit—the shouts, the footsteps, the gunshots—had also vanished.

Over the course of the night two more German convoys passed—one consisting of three cars, and the other, of five military trucks no doubt loaded with soldiers in pursuit.

How much time had passed since she'd left the cave? Thirty minutes? An hour? Three? Off in the east, the sky was just beginning to wake up, and the deep blue of the night was giving way to the pink and azure hues of early morning. Julia's mind clouded with fatigue and above all, cold. She no longer felt her feet, which had become two unwieldy masses of dead, swollen flesh attached to her ankles. She still has some sensation in her fingers, but this was only because she'd kept them plunged into her armpits, which themselves had begun to lose their warmth. Her lips obeyed none of her commands to move, her ears clung lifeless to her deadened skull, and her face had become a frozen mask. Worst of all, she shivered no more. "When your body stops shivering," she recalled Gustaw once telling her while out working in the frozen fields collecting firewood, "that's when you're really in trouble. That means your body's shutting down."

She had to do something. And she had to do it now, or she would die there on the side of the road.

In a growing hypothermic daze, her mind whirled about searching for a plan. Go back up to the cave? No, she'd put the others at risk. Walk down the road? No. For one, she didn't think she could walk anymore. And for another, she'd be spotted and arrested by the first passing convoy. Hail down a driver? But who? The first car that wasn't a German? She looked at the sky. Dawn was approaching. The odds that someone else would drive by in the morning were much greater than someone driving by during the night. With the curfew and the escape, she couldn't imagine any of the farmers in the area risking being on the road. But it was the only chance she had. A risk, yes, but her other option was to freeze to death. Or be spotted by the Germans and arrested, tortured, and killed.

This thought flew through her mind along with images of the operations beyond the wire: naked men, women, and children being herded into the gas chamber, which the Germans had fitted to look like showers. The canisters of Zyklon B—a highly toxic, industrial pesticide—being dropped into the chambers by Ukrainian guards through closeable vents in the roof. The screams—at first wailing and heartrending, but then fading into groans, a few sobs, and silence. Screams that Julia had been tasked with hiding from the rest of the camp by swatting at a herd of wingless geese held just outside the chambers. Over their honking and shrieking, the Germans had hoped that the prisoners' screams would be camouflaged from the rest of the camp and the world. The vents being opened and the gas being expelled from the chamber. The piles of bodies, some still writhing, and others covered in excrement as the condemned had lost control of their bowels in their final moments. The S.S. wading into the human mass and shooting those who were still moving in the head. The *coups de grâce*. And then, the thirty or forty prisoners of the *Sonderkommando* hauling the bodies from the gas chamber and wheeling them on carts to the crematorium beyond the wire, where in groups of three at a time, the bodies would be shoved into perpetually burning ovens, their bones, organs, muscles, and sinews reduced to ash and smoke that wound its way from the towering chimneys away, away, away from this Hell and upwards to Heaven.

Would Julia end up passing through the chimneys as well?

No.

She would fight.

Far off to the left, the sound of an approaching engine yanked her from her trance. She snapped her head to the side, squinting her eyes down the winding road to where it disappeared around a bend. The coming dawn traced a clearer outline of the land's features, but all still glowed a dim black and white. Above, the stars had begun to fade and retreat into the other hemisphere.

As the engine's rumble grew, a paroxysm of terror shot through Julia's limbs, making them scream silently despite the cold. What if this was the Germans coming back? What if they had seen her when they'd passed by and had only been waiting for more light to come back and arrest her? What if they were just toying with her, like some sadistic cat getting ready to pounce on its debilitated prey?

As nonsensical as these ideas were, they seemed perfectly logical in Julia's weakened and feverish mind. No sooner had she lost herself to these panicked thoughts than the vehicle emerged from around the bend, and she saw a rusted and dilapidated Stetysz truck trundling down the road, its bed piled high with firewood. In the growing glare of the early morning, Julia couldn't make out who was behind the wheel, but whoever it was had not seen her in her hiding spot. The truck continued to rumble, sputter, and jerk forward.

A wave of desperate hope pounded Julia from her blind.

She stood.

Her legs screamed but her feet remained mute.

She stumbled, her arms outstretched. She tumbled towards the road. Between her legs, the dried blood scraped the insides of her thighs. Her head spun. Her feet pounded forward. She heard herself speak, scream—a piercing, raspy cry erupting from her broken soul.

Through watering and stinging eyes, she saw the blurry and nondescript form of the truck stop, the aging brakes squealing and piercing her tingling eardrums. *Clump, clump, clump*—with each step her wooden prisoner's clogs rapped against the frigid asphalt, which rushed up to greet her, slowly, slowly, as if she were falling from a great height. Like a massive wall being driven at her with the force of a tank, the road slammed into her fading body. Her head pounded the asphalt with a dull thud.

Ahead of her, a human form stepped from the truck.

She smiled.

She closed her eyes.
All went silent.

четыре

FOUR

"IS HE DEAD?"

The farmer stepped down from the horse-drawn cart and walked over to the body. Clutching his axe in his right hand, he slowed his pace as he neared. It was a man. Clothed in a gray-and-blue striped uniform, he lay facedown in the field, his legs bent backwards as if he'd collapsed while running. His left arm was tucked under his body, and his right lay extended on the ground, grasping for something just out of reach. A half meter from his extended hand, a German pistol lay wedged in the mud. It had clearly fallen with a great deal of force.

"Papa, can you see anything?" Paul stood in the

cart, clutching the horse's reins as he called to his father. When they'd come across the body, Paul had wanted to climb down and look as well, but Rodion thought he was too young. To which Paul had scoffed.

"You stay there," Rodion answered, holding up his free palm. Standing up straight, he scanned the morning horizon. Only fields and forest met his gaze. He stepped forward and leaned over the body.

"It looks like a prisoner! And escaped, I expect," he said, speaking just loud enough for his fifteen-year-old son to hear. But the moment he spoke, he jerked his head up and looked around, terrified that someone—that Germans—might be watching. "And he's dead . . . no, wait!"

Rodion squatted to look more closely at the prisoner. The man seemed to be in his late teens or early twenties, but despite his young age his body looked as if it weighed no more than fifty or sixty kilos. The man's joints and bones pushed against the grayish, almost powdery skin, giving the impression of a skeleton covered in shrinking cloth. The top left-hand corner of his uniform was fouled with blackish blood that had flowed down the man's back and over his side. A small hole in the uniform's shoulder betrayed the source: he had been shot in the shoulder and bled out.

Laying his axe on the ground, Rodion placed his hands on the dirt and leaned over, his face now just feet over the man's body. No, he hadn't been mistaken. The man's throat quivered with the faint pressure of blood moving through his veins.

He wasn't dead.

A surge of fear coursed through Rodion's fifty-year-old body, warming him against the cold morning air. With a trembling arm, he reached forward and placed his hand on the prisoner's shoulder. Warmth. Ever so slight, but warmth greeted his fingers. He slid his hand forward, clutched the man's unwounded arm, and shook firmly but gently. Like a child lost in deep sleep, the man's arms and torso wobbled, but he gave no response. Rodion scanned the man and noticed that his hands had become blue.

Rodion pulled once more, this time rolling the prisoner over so that he could see the man's face. The prisoner was young and thin with freckles and black-rimmed glasses held in place by angular features and an aquiline nose. His closed eyelids were speckled behind a cloudy, filthy mess. On the left breast of his uniform, an inverted red triangle was affixed below a black identification number in German *Frakturschrift*: 1031211. The same insignia marked the man's left pants leg.

As Rodion examined the man, he felt a wave of burning hatred fill his body—a hatred that had been growing ever since the Germans had occupied Poland four years before. Since then, he'd always chosen to keep to himself and his family, preferring to mind his own business on his barley and potato farm, and trying not to go noticed by anyone—his neighbors, the Polish administration, and of course the Germans. From time to time he'd heard about the activities of the Polish Underground—a secret but organized force that worked to both demoralize and weaken the enemy, all the while keeping the Poles' national spirit and hope alive. He'd also heard stories of what happened to suspected Underground members if they were ever caught: interrogation, torture, and execution. Even worse, he knew that the Germans had adopted a heartless system of what they called "collective responsibility," which led them to brutally punish Poles almost at random in the wake of any kind of act of resistance or sabotage. Once, the Germans had all but wiped out an entire village in retaliation for an assassination attempt on one of their officers. Knowing the risks to himself, his family, and village, Rodion had chosen the path of least resistance.

But seeing this man now in his field, Rodion's nerves snapped and his suppressed anger reached its tipping point. It blinded him, it disgusted him, and it transformed him.

He could be passive no longer.

Standing up straight, he turned back to his cart. His eyes darted over the fields and countryside, his heart leaping at anything that seemed to stand out from the slumbering farmland.

"Son, come help me," he said, his voice wavering. "This man's alive. Not by much, but he's alive. I'll be goddamned if I'm going to give the Germans the satisfaction of having even one more victim to their wickedness. Come on! Let's take him home."

ПЯТЬ
FIVE

JÓZEF TURNED ONTO HIS SIDE AND JERKED AWAKE, feeling the cold stone wall of the cave press against his cheek. Sitting up, he massaged his arms and legs and rubbed his torso with both hands, trying to bring warmth back to his body. Sunlight trickled into the cave, blocked only by Russ's body and the tangle of briars hanging outside the cave's entrance. Russ was still hunched over his rifle and peering out. Józef looked around.

"Where's—?"

"Gone," Russ interrupted. "She was gone when I woke up. God knows where. Or why."

Józef leaned forward and tried to peer over Russ's shoulders and toward the road and fields outside.

"Why would she do that? When, hm? Does not she know that—"

"I'm sure she does," Russ interrupted once more, his voice testy. "But she's gone. The sun's up. And here we are with no food, no water, no warm clothes." He lowered the rifle. "And one bullet."

Józef sat back on his haunches and sighed. His thoughts swirled around the past years, during which he'd grown to know Julia in the hell of KL Himmelweg. And now she was gone. With no good-bye. Nothing. Was she even still alive? He leaned forward once more and peeked around Russ's body, almost expecting to see her dead body lying out near the road or in one of the fields that stretched out below them. *She's lost so much blood*, he thought, *there's no way she's got any chance out here by herself. Not like that.* He shook his head and ran his hands over his face and scalp, which had just begun to prickle with new hair.

Since the war started, and especially since he'd arrived in the camp, he'd seen so much death he hardly had any tears or emotion left. As if his body had become little more than a hollow shell of the human he once was. Ana, Pani Hacek, Sławomir, Kazik, Éric: all gone and for what? Like his arms and legs, his heart had grown numb. His blood flowed, his lungs breathed, but his emotions had expired long ago.

"So, now what?" he asked the American, shaking his head. "We cannot stay here. We shall die from cold or starvation. Or we shall be found. We cannot be more than two or three kilometers from camp, hm."

"Right," Russ said. "I fell asleep last night. But I meant to stay up." He swore in anger. "Several German convoys and cars have driven by since I woke up about a half hour ago. But I ain't heard any more voices or shots."

"What is Germans' plan, do you think?"

Russ leaned forward and looked out, turning

his head left and right to see farther up and down the road.

"Well," he sighed, "they probably combed these woods up till the road. But quite frankly I'm surprised they never looked back. Otherwise they'da found this place. Flippin' idiots. My bet is now they're goin' to set up roadblocks and start searchin' the houses and villages all around here—that is, if there are any. I'd spec' their first suspicion would be to see if any farmers or anyone else might be hidin' someone. Like us. Or some of the other prisoners. Or else the Krauts check the roads and train stations."

Russ sat back and turned to Józef. "How many you think got out?"

"I do not know," the Pole answered. "Maybe one hundred?"

Russ shook his head.

"That seems like a lot. From where I was under the sortin' shed I saw *maybe* sixty or so. An' half of them were shot 'fore they got through the wire."

"How well can that many hide, hm?"

Russ shrugged.

"Who knows? I reckon some have been found already."

Silence. The two men sat lost in their thoughts, their eyes easing their way to the cave floor.

"Look," Russ said, causing Józef to snap from his daze, "before I got caught, I was workin' with some partisans—Polish fighters who said they were with the Underground. Over near a town called Zeberka, I think."

"So?"

"So . . . they were armed and bands of 'em were all over. In the east, in the middle, you name it. Working from farms, houses, and even settin' up camps hidden in the woods. I only worked with a few, but they told me that there must've been thousands of men and women from all over takin' part. Armed. Ready to fight against the Germans."

"We should find them, do you think?"

"Yep, that's exactly what I am saying. We can't

stay here—we know that much. And it'd be stupid to go to any town or even follow the road. So," he pointed through the cave door at a forest that lay a hundred meters away, on the other side of the field facing them. "That way's east. If we can make it to that wood over there, we'll have some cover. We move east until . . . "

"Until?"

"Until we either find the partisans or end up in Russia. Which can't be too far, I reckon. At least based on what I can remember before I was brought in."

Józef looked at the American. "Should we wait until dark? Is it not risky to move around during daytime?"

"Of course it's risky. And we'd need to cross that field to make it to the forest. But if we stay here, we'll both end up stone cold dead before night falls. We need to move. If anythin' to stay warm."

"Well, let us stop talking and we go." Józef

patted Russ on the back and nodded toward the entrance.

Leaning forward, Russ pushed the brambles aside with his hand and looked out. He paused and then inched out farther until he could lift his leg and step outside. As he moved, he clutched the rifle across his chest, ready to fire if need be. He looked down the embankment to the left and toward the road. Then to the right. He stopped. Behind him, Józef followed until both men stood just outside of the cave's entrance. When Józef was out, Russ let go of the bushes, which flopped back into place, hiding the cave. Even someone just meters away would have trouble seeing the entrance.

"How did you see this?" Józef whispered.

Russ turned around and looked at the briars. He shrugged.

"Dunno. I saw somethin' a little too dark behind the bush from where we were standin'. Good luck, I guess."

"Hm."

Keeping their eyes peeled on the road and the surrounding countryside, the American and the Pole eased their way down the embankment and toward the road. Russ's toes screamed in agony with each step. The frigid night had all but frozen them, but as he moved he began to regain more and more feeling. He wondered if any of his toes was frostbitten. But now was not the time to worry about toes. They had to cross a field and get to cover.

When Russ and Józef reached the drainage ditch beside the road, they paused, listening and watching. Satisfied no cars were coming, Russ jerked his right arm forward and bounded up and across the asphalt, with Józef close behind. Their wooden prisoner's clogs rattled against the hard surface, sending a silence-shattering rapping over the two-laned expanse. They crossed into the field beyond the road. Russ ran as best he could, holding the rifle out in front of him like a tightrope walker's balancing pole. His head darted left and right while his eyes scanned every corner of the field, all the while returning again and again to their goal: the forest that was still a hundred meters away.

Both Russ and Józef ran with their heads ducked, as if by doing so they could hide from the sun that beat down on them, exposing them to the entire countryside. All it would take for their journeys to end suddenly and violently would be for one car to drive by. Like two animated scarecrows, they waltzed across the field in their gray-and-blue striped uniforms, their arms held high as if running across hot coals. Both Russ's and Józef's nerves were stretched to their limit, for they were exposed to the world and little more than moving targets.

Fifty meters to go.

Thirty.

Twenty.

While running, both men wheezed from the effort, their breath coming in short, violent bursts. Even though their years of working in the quarry had added definition to their muscles, malnutrition had sapped their bodies of any real physical benefit of the exercise. They were worn down and weak, and now they were pushing their bodies and their minds to the brink of their endurance.

Ten meters.

Five.

Despite the cold winter air, when they reached the shade of the forest, the two men collapsed in a heap onto the ground, reveling in the shade as if they'd just run through a desert in search of solace from the heat. Lying on their backs with their arms limp over their chests and at their sides, the men's bodies heaved with exhaustion—up and down, up and down, up and down their stomachs inflated and deflated with lightning speed, like some mal-functioning mechanical bellows. They hissed and gurgled to catch their breath, their heads lolling back and forth as both men continued to look behind them to make sure that no one had seen or followed them.

The field was empty.

The road, bare.

"Come on," Russ interrupted their panting and stood. "Let's move."

With a nod, Józef pushed himself into a sitting position and paused, his head spinning from the sudden upright movement. When his vision had cleared and the dizziness had faded, he leaned forward and pushed himself up with his hands. Shaking the tingling from his legs, he turned and followed the American deeper into the Polish forest in search of partisan fighters.

шесть
SIX

"WHAT ARE YOU DOING? SHE CAN'T STAY HERE!"

"Father, please. This is the only place in the village she'd be safe. In the crypt. It's the most hidden I can think of where we could get her better."

"The crypt! The Gestapo have been all over Piekło! They're looking for the escaped prisoners."

"But father, you are respected here. Surely they'll—"

"Surely nothing! They've been here three times already!"

Two soupy voices swirled over Julia. Drifting in and out of consciousness, she registered the voices of two men. They were familiar voices, but ones she hadn't heard since long before her arrest.

When she opened her eyes, she felt warmth.

For the first time in years, comfortable sheets enveloped her body, which lay nestled upon a mattress as soft as down. Not a ticking mattress filled with flea- and chigger-infested straw that poked and jabbed at every turn. No, this was an actual mattress. And she was wrapped in actual, thick comforters and sheets, her head resting upon a feather pillow. Her arms and legs bathed in warmth, and her fingers and toes once again felt like part of her body.

Gone were the wooden, straw-lined, overcrowded bunks of KL Himmelweg.

"How do you feel? Can you hear me?" A man's voice spoke somewhere above her. Looking up, she discerned a blurry figure leaning over her. She blinked, pulled her hands from under the covers, and rubbed her eyes. Slowly the man's figure came into focus. Standing at the head of the bed, he smiled, his head and shoulders upside down from her perspective.

"Matthiew?" she asked, trying to sit up. But her strength failed her and she slumped back into the bed.

The peasant placed his hand on her forehead.

"Yes, Julia, it is I," he answered, his voice soothing and warm. "You are back in Piekło." He tapped her forehead gently, as if calming a small child. "You are in the church. Father Witold is here, too."

"But . . . Piekło . . . how?" Tears welled up in Julia's eyes. She looked at Matthiew, an unshaven, weathered man of about sixty. He was dressed in ragged leather breeches and a worn flannel shirt bulging from underneath a corduroy hunting jacket. He clutched a faded brown hat in both hands, his fingers working over the cloth as he fumbled with his words. His eyes smiled at her, despite apparent years of suffering and worry.

At first, she didn't recognize where she was: a small, four-by-five meter room with stucco walls and a large crucifix hanging at the far end. On either side of the wistful Savior's porcelain form, two thick, red candles burned silently, their flames sending a calming glow down their waxen shafts. Underneath the crucifix sat a cushioned hassock for kneeling and praying. To its right stood a small wooden lectern supporting a thick, leather-bound Bible. To the left of the Bible, Father Witold wavered, one hand on the book. His face was stern, and when she looked at him he lowered his eyes. This was not the same kind face she'd always known growing up. The priest looked different—haggard, weather-beaten, and overcome with worry.

"Am I . . . ?"

"You are in the church's sacristy, here in Piekło," Witold hissed defensively, his voice barely audible. "*He* brought you here."

"Do you remember me?" Matthiew's raucous voice echoed from next to her bed.

Julia eased her head up and gazed at him, lost in memories that had been suppressed long ago. The man glanced at the priest, who once more furrowed his heavyset brows. Julia searched the recesses of her mind.

She started.

"Matthiew?"

Matthiew smiled and kneeled, bringing his face level with hers.

"So you *do* remember me? I'm the one who brought you to Gustaw along with your brother, Otto, all those years ago. And can you imagine? I was transporting some firewood just four days ago and there you came, walking out of the woods, wearing a prisoner's uniform and covered in blood. You passed out. Right there in the street. It was only when I got out of the truck and came over to look that I recognized you."

Matthiew paused, breathing the deep, emphysemic rattle of a lifelong chain-smoker. "So I brought you here. Before . . . I mean, before the war, I saw you and your brother around about and what-not, only . . . " He looked down at his hands.

Julia couldn't see them but could tell from the movement of his shoulders that he was wringing his hat.

"Only," he continued, "when you and Otto disappeared several years ago, everyone thought you were dead. Even Gustaw."

"Gustaw!" Julia managed to sit up, despite her weakness. At her sudden movement, Witold stepped to her side and placed his hand behind her back to steady her. "Where is he? How is he? Why isn't he here? Can we go see him? I have to let him know I'm alive!"

Matthiew and Witold exchanged glances. Matthiew averted his eyes.

"He's gone," Witold snapped. "After you and your brother had vanished, he . . . he . . . " Acid filled his voice, as if he were glad that Gustaw were gone.

"What?" Julia asked, her voice impatient. She gazed at the priest, trying to understand why his tone felt so hostile.

"He became lost in drink," Witold said. "People heard him crying out in the night. And then no more. He drank himself to death."

Julia sank back down into the pillow, squeezing her eyes shut tight. Salty drops glistened from underneath her lids. Suppressing deep, guttural sobs, she brought her hand up to hide her face from the two men.

"What happened to Otto?" Matthiew asked.

Julia just shook her head in reply, her body trembling from the weight of sorrow. After a few silent minutes had passed, she squeezed the last tears from her eyes and blinked again, looking first to Matthiew and then to Witold.

"And the house? Gustaw's house?"

"Germans," the priest answered. "Since Gustaw died, there was no one to inherit. No one from around here to take over. We'd talked about it amongst ourselves, but the Germans were faster. And stronger. They took over Gustaw's house and moved in. With some children, too. And now the

Germans are *everywhere*. And they are looking for people from that camp. For you." He looked down at her with piercing eyes. Her flesh crept under his unblinking gaze. She withered under her sheets and turned her eyes to Matthiew.

"Listen," Witold continued. "Matthiew brought you here a few days ago. Since then the Germans have poured through the village. Said they were looking for prisoners who'd escaped. We all heard the shots. We all know what's been going on over there in the forest. Everyone knows." He paused, taking a deep breath. "They'll come back. You can't stay here."

A pang of terror welled up deep in Julia's bosom.

He looked around, his eyes lingering on the stained and glistening crucifix. "Only Matthiew and I know you're here. But that can't last. We're going to move you to the crypt. For now. But," he looked up at Matthiew. "*Matthiew* will find another place. Elsewhere."

Matthiew shuffled in place. "But father, what about—" he began.

"What about *nothing*!" The priest snapped. "We've discussed this. I've decided."

Matthiew gave Witold a withering look. His face flushed crimson. He took several deep, hissing breaths to calm himself. He shifted his tongue around in his mouth, as if forming his words. He turned his eyes to Julia.

"You know," Matthiew said, changing the subject, "this can't last much longer. This war. The Allies have landed in France and Italy, and the Soviets are moving in from the east. Hitler's being squeezed to death. It's just a matter of time before the two armies meet and this is all over." He looked upward and crossed himself.

On the other side of the bed, Witold made a spitting noise and muttered something under his breath. "Let me get you something to eat," Witold said, his voice suddenly soothing. "It's not much, vegetables in broth. But it should help you to get your strength back."

He climbed the steps and returned several minutes later with a plate holding a steaming bowl. Wincing, Julia pulled herself up and looked at Witold. Her eyes expressed her thanks, but her soul felt apprehensive. What was he thinking? Why was he being so resistant to her hiding in the church? What had the Germans said to him? He walked to the side of her bed and sat the tray down onto her upper legs. He glanced at Matthiew and nodded.

Julia lifted a trembling spoon of broth to her chapped and ashen lips. She slurped the soup in drop by drop. The warmth felt scalding compared with the cold she'd endured over the past year. The soup slid down to her stomach and a new energy radiated to her limbs and torso. Was life returning? She took another sip and closed her eyes. Her body warmed, and she smiled.

SEVEN
семь

WHEN ÉRIC AWOKE, THE OVERPOWERING SMELL OF HAY filled his nostrils, its thick dust fouling the air and tickling his windpipe. Where the hell was he? His thoughts drifted to the path that had gotten him here. As a student in Lyon, he had printed anti-Vichy flyers, sabotaged German trucks, been tortured by the Gestapo, ridden in a cattle car train across Europe, managed to survive a year in the death camp, then escaped, stealing the pistol off a dead Ukrainian guard as he ran. Groggy and dizzy, he shook his head to fight off the memories.

Éric opened his eyes and jerked about in a fit of coughing, each lurch of his body sending waves of pain radiating out from his shoulder like fiery knives. Aside from a few weak but jagged lines of light dancing around him, all was dark. His body trembled with waves of convulsive shivering—not that he was cold, but he burned with a fever that seared his mind and stung his eyes. Sweat covered his body. His clothes stuck to his torso, his arms, his legs. His throat bulged and squeezed shut as if stuffed with cotton. He tried to smack his lips to work up some spit, but none came. His mouth felt like a filthy sock that had dried in the wind and lost all of its softness.

Éric sat up. His head hit the solid and prickly mass of bound hay that formed the ceiling of whatever cramped space he was lying in. The impact sent waves of throbbing pain through his head, neck, and shoulders. Searing pain originating in his left shoulder, which felt swollen and detached from the rest of his body. He clutched his eyes and forehead with his unwounded right hand and tried to look around. He lifted his hand and felt around the spot where he lay.

Underneath his body, several layers of thick wool blankets formed an improvised pallet that cushioned him from what lay underneath. Shifting his rear and his legs, he sensed that he was positioned on several tightly bound stacks of hay that had been pushed together. He was in a small enclosure fashioned entirely of hay: the floor, the walls, the ceiling. As if someone had made a hidden fort and placed him inside. In the dark. Was he in a barn somewhere? He had to be.

Éric's breath came in short gasps and echoed off the sides, bottom, and top of his improvised bunker. Judging from the echo and hollowness of the sound of his own breathing and shifting in place, his enclosure was about the size of four coffins stacked two-by-two on top of each other. The thick, grassy smell of rotting hay was overpowering.

Éric squinted his eyes tight. Images and sounds from the past day rocketed through his mind: the buzzing camp transformer; the distracted guard just above in the watchtower; the crowbar thrown across the bushings; the massive, ear-shattering pop and blinding shower of sparks; the gunshots; the smoke rising above the camp; his running through the wire and across the field; the burning bullet ripping through his left shoulder from behind, before he even heard the rifle's report. Despite the pain and the blood coursing down his back and chest from the exit wound, he had run through the field and into the wood, over brambles and roots, around trees, and back out of the wood and into another field.

Then everything had faded to black as the shorn grass rushed up to meet him.

With his left arm crippled, Éric stretched himself out onto his back and planted his feet into the sides of his hay enclosure. Grunting and sweating, he pushed. The wall budged slightly and his thighs shook with the effort. Exhausted, he relaxed his legs, and the hay shifted back into place. Éric's head spun. When he regained his strength, he tried again, this time pushing against the ceiling. All that happened this time was that a flurry of hay dust and dead chiggers drifted down onto his face, where they stuck to his clammy skin. His heart and lungs pounded against his ribs as if he'd just finished a marathon. What was happening to him?

From outside of his makeshift hideaway, a crack snapped him from his trance. He held his breath and, despite the dark, turned his eyes to the right— where the sound had come from. He squinted into the black. Nothing. A rustle. Some footsteps.

Someone was coming.

His heart leapt once again to his throat. He pulled his right hand down to his waist. He ran his trembling palm over his belt, looking for the pistol he'd found during the escape, and Éric had clutched throughout his fight. It was gone. Feeling panic sweeping into his hay cave, Éric rolled onto his side and swept his arm around, looking for the weapon. But nothing—only hay and more hay.

Snap!

Éric froze, listening. The pounding of his heart deafened him.

More footsteps. The wall of hay shook as if someone just outside had punched or kicked it. It shifted. Someone was pulling it out of place—sliding it out like the piece of a giant, three-dimensional puzzle. Around the edge of the bale, a crack of white light pushed through into the dark, forming a blinding, jagged rectangle. Éric rotated his body and leaned back, pulling his knees to his chest, ready to kick at whomever was coming for him. He may have been unarmed, but he would not die without fighting. He'd already survived Gestapo torture back in France, he'd survived an escape from a Nazi death camp, and he was determined to survive whatever search committee the Germans had sent out into the Polish countryside looking for him and the other escapees.

With a rustle and soft crunch, the bale slid from its spot, flooding Éric in light.

"*Dzień dobry*," a soft, young man's voice greeted him from outside. "*Czy czujesz się lepiej?*"

Éric squinted at his visitor. Whoever it was, he was speaking Polish. Not German. In Éric's years in the camp, he'd picked up a few Polish words, but knew far more German, since that was the language of the camp. That and Yiddish. Whoever it was, his tone of voice was not that of someone who had come to arrest him.

"*Halo?*" Éric ventured. As his eyes adjusted to the light, the person's form came into view. He was a boy of about fourteen or fifteen, with dark, unkempt hair and the beginnings of a beard. His eyes were black and shone with a deep, internal fire. The boy was clearly a peasant: he wore torn work pants and a filthy cotton top. A pair of brown suspenders held up his pants. A bulky, unwieldy vest protected his body from the cold, which swept in to greet Éric like a bucket of frigid water. His body in the enclosed space had created a sort of oven that kept him warm and protected from the Polish winter.

"I am Paul," the boy said in Polish. This time Éric understood.

"I am Éric."

Paul nodded and smiled. Bending over, he disappeared from view, retrieving something he'd left below. At the same time he allowed Éric to see outside.

Surrounded by mountains of hay—some in rectangular bundles, some in carefully assembled stacks—Éric saw that he was in a large barn with open sides all around. Apparently for storing hay. Apart from the hay, the barn stored no tools, carts, tractors, or animals—what Éric would've otherwise expected to see on a farm. Beyond the barn's walls, the flat countryside stretched out in all directions, broken about a kilometer away by the rough outline of a forest. Was that where he'd run? Yesterday? Two days ago? Éric realized that he had no idea how much time had gone by since the escape. He'd been unconscious all this time. But at least a day had passed. A light blanket of snow had appeared, and silent, wistful flakes were drifting from the gray clouds.

Paul's head reappeared, causing Éric to start. The Pole lifted a steaming bowl and placed it on the hay in front of the Frenchman. He then produced a spoon and a half loaf of black bread. The smell of rutabaga and cabbage drifted over Éric's face. His stomach howled an answer.

"*Dziękuję*, thank you," Éric nodded, reaching out for the soup. As he did, his eyes fell on his left shoulder, which was now bandaged with several layers of cotton and burlap. Following Éric's gaze with his eyes, Paul said something, nodding at the bandage. He pointed and gesticulated, but Éric understood only the words *bad*, *blood*, and *death*. Or was it *dead*?

Éric looked back up. The two locked gazes for a moment, as if trying to understand each other without words. While Paul was right there, Éric hesitated to begin eating. Soon Paul broke the silence.

"Eat." He nodded toward the bowl. Éric lifted the spoon and sipped. The faint reek of rotten vegetables warmed his mouth and throat as he swallowed. He took several more sips before biting into the bread, which was a mixture of rye dough and sawdust. Now that he had replaced some of the fluid in his mouth, he chewed slowly before forcing the mush down. Paul reached over and tapped Éric on the hand. Now, he was simplifying his sentences, reducing them to single words and a flurry and hand movements.

"You. Gestapo. Bad. No. Camp. No. Bad."

Paul stepped back, measuring the impact of his words. Éric nodded. Paul pointed once again at the Frenchman.

"You. Here. Me. Papa." He paused and looked over his shoulder, as if indicating where his father might be. Perhaps in a nearby house? Perhaps in the fields working? Paul turned back to Éric.

"Here. Gestapo. No. *NO!* Here. You. Live."
He reached forward and patted Éric on the healthy
shoulder. He smiled, nodding at the food and then
at Éric's wounded arm.

"You. Live."

EIGHT

"**Z**EBERKA," RUSS WHISPERED, SQUINTING THROUGH THE deepening gloom of the approaching night. He nestled closer to the massive elder tree and hugged his rifle against his chest. Józef stepped up behind him, his feet crunching through the crusty frost. Though it had been snowing since morning, Józef and Russ's constant movement had been the only thing keeping hypothermia away. But as they stopped to survey the approaching village, the aching sting that shot up through his legs and into his spine told Russ that his feet had not been so lucky. With only the camp's wooden prisoner clogs for protection, frostbite was destroying his toes and feet.

"Zeberka?" Józef asked, peering over Russ's shoulder. "How do you know? You are not from here. You are not Pole."

"Before I was caught I was brought through here," the American answered. "It was a rendezvous point with the partisans. And I recognize it. Maybe some of them are still here." He gazed at the village, which opened up in front of them and slightly below as the ground sloped away from them. Since they'd fled the camp, their entire journey had inched downhill. The village consisted of little more than two or three dozen decrepit farm buildings, their aging, pink-and-orange stucco peeling from their walls and crumbling into growing piles at the foundations. Bullet holes pockmarked some of the walls and façades. Russ couldn't remember the bullet holes from before. He wondered at what kind of violence the town had seen since he'd passed through.

Since the war had started. Since the Germans had taken it upon themselves to work through every village, town, and city in Poland in their quest to make the whole country *Judenrein*—free of Jews. Since he'd arrived at KL Himmelweg, Russ had heard the word tossed around with hatred. How could Hitler possibly hope to get rid of *all* the Jews? Why would he even want to do such a thing? He shook his head and squinted at the comatose buildings. Even though no sounds or movement emerged from Zeberka, he knew the Poles were keeping themselves behind closed doors. Especially now that night was falling and the German-imposed curfew was approaching.

"What do we do, hm?" Józef asked.

Sitting up, Russ looked down at his uniform and sighed. "Whatever we do, people will know right away who we are. And I'd be willin' to bet that the Germans are either snoopin' around or have moles everywhere just dyin' to put their hands on any money that might be offered to catch us. We need to see if there are partisan contacts here. But we really need civilian clothes before we can do much and hope not to get caught."

"How about that?" Józef pointed down to one small farmhouse nestled off to the village's right, like a loner among a crowd of popular kids in a school playground. The house's ground-floor windows cast a yellowish glow on the snow-covered field that reached up to the front door. Russ followed Józef's gaze.

"They might have something, hm."

"But what? We ain't got any money. And what if they turn us in? Or call the Germans? Or shoot us on the spot?"

Józef looked at Russ's chest.

"What about that?" he pointed to the rifle, which dimly reflected the crescent moonlight. Night had completely fallen.

"What? Trade it?" A violent frisson racked Russ's body.

"What other choice do we have? Die of cold?

Look at you. You are blue. And I am sure that I am, too. And what is greater risk: trying to fight off Germans with one bullet? Germans that recognize us a kilometer away? Or try to blend in? And maybe they have some food. And look," he pointed off above Zeberka's rooftops and into the distance.

In the dying light, Russ could just make out the snaking form of a silent river.

"You see that?" Józef continued. "That is Bug River. Ukraine is on other side. And I am sure the Red Army cannot be far. Or maybe partisans. If we blend in, we could—"

"Okay, okay, you've convinced me," Russ interrupted. "It's that or die of cold. Let's go. You do the talkin'. You're the Polack."

With pained, creaking knees, the two men stood.

His head spinning from the sudden effort, Russ steadied himself against the tree. His breath came in short, shallow huffs. When his vision had cleared and his head regained a modicum of composure, he clutched the rifle and stepped forward.

They were two exposed prisoners trudging across the Polish countryside.

When the two men reached to within fifty yards of the house, where a low hedge marked the beginning of the property, Józef laid his hand on Russ's shoulder and squeezed. The American stopped and turned around.

"You wait here," Józef said. "I shall go see. If something happens to me, you might have chance."

Russ nodded and stepped up to the hedge. He squatted. Józef stepped up to the house, his feet *crunch, crunch, crunch, crunching* in the thickening snow. Russ lowered his head below the top of the hedge. He was now—he thought—invisible to anyone in the house, but he could still peer through the plant and watch Józef's movements. Every few minutes he looked around behind him to make sure that he was alone. Even though the village seemed to sleep, he couldn't afford the risk of a passing farmer or patrol spotting him.

Knockknockknock.

Józef rapped against the door. Russ's nerves cracked. The knocking annihilated the silence. Russ felt as if the sound were calling the entire village and German army to look at them, as if a spotlight were being cast directly on them. His panicked heartbeat echoed the sound of Józef's knuckles against the aged wood.

Silence.

Józef stepped back from the door and looked around, as if trying to see if anyone might be leaning out one of the windows to peer at him. He stepped up and knocked again.

A thump and scrape from inside. Another.

Russ crouched down closer to the ground and slid his finger to the rifle's trigger.

The door opened and the shadow of a woman appeared. Squinting through the hedge, Russ made out the hunched-over form of an old woman. White hair escaping from underneath a headscarf, knitted wool tricot folded over the woman's aged shoulders, flowered apron, bulging and fluffy slippers. Like a broken radio her voice crackled over the distance between them, the Polish syllables forming an impenetrable fog. Józef spoke. The woman peered over his shoulders nervously. Her body language betrayed her fear. She crossed her arms and shifted in place, hardly making eye contact with her shadowy visitor. She listened. Józef explained. He moved his hands up and down, back and forth. He pointed. He paused. He lowered his head like a beaten dog. Józef seemed to be waiting for the woman to speak. She seemed to be thinking. She shuffled backwards into the house. She looked up. She nodded and beckoned to him.

Józef stepped into the house. The door closed behind him with a click. The sounds disappeared as the two vanished inside. Back in his hiding spot, Russ pulled his arms across his chest in an attempt to preserve some of his body warmth against the biting, excruciating cold. He turned and glanced behind him. Darkness had smothered Zeberka.

A click.

Russ snapped his head back to the house.

The door swung open, and Józef's silhouette appeared in the glowing, rectangular wooden frame. He leaned out and peered into the night, trying to find Russ's hiding spot. He paused, staring. Pinpointing where the American sat hunched and freezing, he waved his right arm, signaling for Russ to come into the house.

Inside, the crackling of a fire in the fireplace chased away the silence and the cold of outside. The warmth melted into Russ's every pore, almost putting him to sleep the moment he stepped in. Every muscle in his body melted. Since he'd been caught by the Nazis two years before, he'd almost forgotten what a comforting home felt like. The sweltering, mosquito-infested heat of the Polish summer, yes, but the soothing, relaxing warmness of a hearth and living room, no. As the heat spread into his body, the urge to urinate swelled over him like a shot of adrenaline. But with a swirling head, Russ sat down on the first chair that offered itself to him, and the need ebbed.

"She says she hates Germans," Józef said, taking a seat across the room from Russ. Russ sat and looked around. The three of them were in a small kitchen off to one side of the house. The orange flames hissing in the stone fireplace filled the room with a sweltering heat, made even more so by the fact that the women had closed the two doors leading from the kitchen and into the rest of the house. Russ guessed that she lived alone and spent most of her time in this small, stuffy room. She eyed Russ with tired yet piercing eyes. The American nodded at her and muttered a weak Polish *thank you* to thank her for letting them in from the cold. As Józef spoke she remained planted like a sentinel in the kitchen doorway.

"They killed her husband," Józef continued. "During one of the *Aktionen*—when the Germans'

Einsatzgruppen came in at the beginning of the war and killed people all over. Anyone suspected of being Jewish or who seemed like they will resist." He paused and caught his breath. The woman kept her eyes riveted on Russ.

"Right after our escape, she says that Germans were everywhere, looking for prisoners. Which is why she let me—us—in. She does not want the gun. She just wants to fight against Germans if she can. In her way. By helping us, she can do that."

Józef turned to the woman and the two exchanged a few sentences in Polish. Russ interrupted, addressing her directly in the little Polish that he could muster.

"Excuse me. Thank you very much. What is your name?"

The woman jerked her head toward Russ, apparently shocked that he could speak Polish. Her expression was one of wonder, like a child marveling at an organ grinder's trained monkey. A smile crept across her wrinkled and weather-beaten face. She answered in a rickety, raspy voice. One that spoke quickly and, to Russ, incomprehensibly. Józef nodded, and when she had finished he turned to Russ.

"She does not want to say," he said, keeping his eyes on her as if reassuring her that he was translating accurately. He shifted his gaze toward Russ. "Better that way. If we get caught, then less for us to tell. Under torture."

The woman shuffled from the doorway and across the kitchen to a cupboard that was suspended over a white metallic washbasin. Reaching up, she opened the wooden pantry and pulled out a half loaf of black bread and a package wrapped in paper. She sat the two items on the table in front of the escapees along with a blunt folding knife and turned back around to pull down a clear glass bottle that she sat down on the table with a clink. She then put out two milky glasses.

"Brandy," she said with a glint in her eye. She reached over and unfolded the package. Inside, six round, golden-brown cakes the size of small saucers lay neatly arranged in a line. *Paczki*—Polish donuts. Józef gawked at the sight of the dessert. "Please," she said, motioning to the food, "I made these with some chocolate that a . . . friend was able to get for me. In secret. If you understand what I mean. We do what we can in these times, no? But now you need this more than me." She shuffled back to the doorway, where a small wicker chair sat propped between the door and the fireplace. She sat, emitting a groan that mingled with the creaking of the chair. Russ imagined that this spot was where she spent many of her winter nights—away from the windows, and sheltered near the heat of the flame.

No sooner had the woman sat down than Russ and Józef fell upon the food like famished dogs tearing apart leftovers. Despite his hunger, Russ forced himself to chew slowly. The chocolate sweetness of the donuts tingled in his mouth and over his tongue, which over the past two years had forgotten what sweet tasted like. Tears welled in his eyes. He choked the pastry down, chasing it with the brandy. His throat and esophagus burned as the liquid tumbled into his stomach. Soon, a new warmth spread through his veins and into every corner of his body—the warmth of alcohol and the energy of the sugar. Between bites, Józef exchanged words with the woman, turning to Russ every few sentences to translate. As the Pole spoke, Russ felt his vision and hearing blur and melt into the fog of the brandy, which, coupled with the fatigue and terror of the past week, pushed him closer and closer to sleep.

"We can stay tonight," Józef said, ripping a piece of donut with his teeth, no longer bothering to use the knife. His straining jaw jostled chunks of the brown meat in his mouth while he talked. "But we have to leave tomorrow. Too dangerous to stay. She says partisans have all left Zeberka. They have moved north and east. Where Soviets are. Hm. She thinks our best chance is to cross Bug River and try to reach Russians." He shook his head. "Apparently Americans are coming this way from the west. And

Stalin and Patton have Germans in a big pincer, and they are squeezing Hitler to death. Thank God."

"The Russians?" Russ mumbled in reply. "What do you know about them in this war?" Józef's jaw worked through the tough sausage.

"They are bastards," he answered after swallowing a morsel of the dried meat. "Hitler had already come into Poland in '39 when Stalin came in from east. Like Poles are some goddamned chess game." He looked up as he referenced the game that the two men had played together so many times while in KL Himmelweg.

"But," Józef continued, taking a deep breath and puffing his chest out in defiance. "Stalin is not interested in getting rid of Jews. So between rock and hard place, he is best bet for us."

NINE

ÉRIC SNAPPED AWAKE. HE OPENED HIS EYES AND SAW the familiar blackness of his improvised hay hideout. Images danced in front of his eyes—images he could see, hear, smell, taste, and touch there, in his hay coffin with him. Images of wolves, of cats, of phantoms, interlaced with splashes and sparkles of light and color.

Gangrene was searing his brain into a hallucinogenic frenzy. Blinking against the visions, Éric grimaced against the riveting, scissoring pain that thrust out from his shoulder and through his body. His entire body trembled with fever and delirium. Sweat covered his torso and soaked his clothes, which had begun to reek of body odor, urine, and shit.

But now there was something else. Some new smell. Like meat left out to rot.

Another lancet of fire ripped through his shoulder and torso.

"Aaaaaagggggghhhh!" he clenched his teeth against the pain, trying to hold back the sound of his scream, which reverberated in his skull. He writhed, arching his back against the woolen palette underneath him, which buckled and bowed with his thrashing.

Panic.

Claustrophobic terror.

The ceiling and walls were pushing in on him. From all directions, in the dark, in the straw, the air was seeping out from between the individual stacks of hay and filling his lungs with the asphyxiating reek of hay dust and rotting flesh. As if in a coffin and buried alive, he was being squeezed—compressed to death by the weight of five tons of cattle feed.

"AAAAAAHHHHH!" he shrieked again, this time his vocal cords buckling under the pressure and straining to their breaking point. Despite the overwhelming, nauseating pain in his shoulder, arm, and spine, he throttled and kicked out in all directions, determined to beat away his grave and push his way into fresh air and freedom. *Thump, whack, thump, thump.* His arms, elbows, knees, feet, and fists pounded away at the unyielding, itching, stabbing hay. His breathing became more frantic and his heart wrenched to bursting. Fire lanced at him, through him, again and again. His mind had left him. All that remained was the animal instinct to fight, to flee, to get out. Or, as Paul had said, *to live.*

With a bone-crunching kick, the right side of his sarcophagus budged, the haystack sliding a few centimeters. Detecting the lapse in resistance, Éric rotated his entire body around on his rear and delivered kick after two-footed kick, grunting, swearing, and screaming with each blow. Five centimeters. Twenty. The hay moved, moved, moved out, out, out.

At the apex of his effort, Éric hurled his aching and numb feet one last time at his tomb's wall, sending it tumbling out and downward with a muffled, bouncing *thu-thump-thump*.

Against the jolting coldness of the winter air that rushed in over him like an arctic baptism, Éric flailed his arms and his legs backwards at his humid, moldy, reeking enclosure until he tumbled bodily from his hay blind and down a massive stairway formed by stacks of hay, five bales thick. Three meters he tumbled, like a worn rag doll tossed down the stairs by a child, until he collided violently with the straw-strewn, frozen earth below. The impact knocked the wind from his lungs and left him lying flat on his back, his eyes fixed on the ceiling of the storage barn where he'd spent the past three weeks. But for Éric, time had ceased to exist. In his mind, he'd been lodged away in the hay for a day, maybe two. Hidden away in an improvised hay structure made to keep him hidden and warm.

As his breath returned and his vision cleared, Éric closed his eyes and pushed himself up from the ground with his right hand. In all of his life, he'd never experienced pain as agonizing as that which now racked his body. Slowly, slowly, slowly he inched his way up until—after what seemed like many minutes—he sat with his left arm hanging limp in the hay at his side, his right burning from the effort.

When his right arm had regained its strength, he reached his hand up and, in one violent movement, dug his fingers under the cloth bandage swaddling his left shoulder and yanked, ripping the bandage from its place. With a ripping scratch, the cloth dislodged itself from the wound, where it had become affixed as the blood had dried and formed a type of human glue. Like a giant scab being torn from unhealed flesh, the bandage tore apart the muscle and viscera and reopened the festering bullet wound.

The blood flowed again from Éric's shoulder like a saturated sponge being squeezed. He tore the silence of the Polish countryside with an ear-splitting scream. Even when his voice had ceased to cry, the woeful echo reverberated throughout the fields and wood beyond. Panting, Éric clenched his teeth against the pain and looked down at his shoulder.

Just below the joint between his upper arm and the socket, and about three centimeters towards his nipple, a dark, almost black hole smacked at him like a slobbering fish's gullet gaping for air. A steady flow of thick red blood drained from the abscess as syrup drains from the opening of a bottle. In an area the size of his fist, the skin around the hole had become a greenish-white, and had begun to peel away as it rotted. It no longer even resembled flesh. Rather, his entire shoulder looked as though it were made of some shoddy leather that had been left in the sun for weeks.

Balancing his torso in his sitting position, Éric reached his right hand up gingerly, preparing to touch the wound. But his hand froze just centimeters away from his shoulder. Éric blinked. He rubbed his eyes and strained his neck to try and gain a better vantage. Was he delirious? Was he dreaming? Was his wound moving? At such a close and awkward angle, his shoulder seemed little more than a blur of red, blue, green, and black. But through the blur, the perimeter of the wound seemed to writhe and undulate, as if something were pushing against his skin from the inside.

He reached up again. Looking up at the ceiling and preparing for the pain, he felt his way across his chest and to his shoulder, his fingers easing their way across the foreign, slimy landscape that this part of his body had become.

Wet. Smooth. Slippery. Warm. Sticky.

He placed no pressure on his skin as he touched

his wound. He ran his palm across its surface. Aside from the gummy moistness, little bumps danced under his fingertips like constellations of pimples that had peppered his back as a young teenager.

He pulled his hand back and looked down. His head reeled at what he saw.

There, in the middle of his blood-covered, trembling palm, a cluster of small, whitish forms wriggled and writhed.

Maggots.

Making a rancid meal of Éric's rotting flesh.

Before his mind could react to the sight, his stomach knotted painfully, hurling sour liquid up through his throat, mouth, and over his legs. The warmth of Éric's vomit soaked through his prisoner's uniform, creeping around and over his thighs and knees. He coughed. He retched. He vomited again and again, until all that crossed his lips was a belch that reeked of gastric juice. In the cold air, his now wet legs chilled, sending a nauseating tremor through his body. In his fright, Éric slammed his right palm into the hay as if squishing a fly or mosquito. He smashed his hand down again and again, each impact sending waves of pain up into his left shoulder.

In the midst of this panicked spasm, a horrifying thought lurched through Éric's mind and snapped him from his delirium: he had to get up and out of this moving cattle train. Because he was back in the train—the transport from France to Poland. He knew it! He was again one of the human condemned. He would escape, yes, and trudge through the cold, back to the traboules in the old part of Lyon—the secret corridors once used for transporting silk and that were now being used by Resistance members to deliver messages and black-market goods. He had to get out. Now. If he didn't, he would surely end up in some labor or transit camp somewhere, while his Resistance contact would be waiting for him and his delivery.

His delivery.

Where the hell had he put it?

As his gangrenous hallucination intensified, Éric elbowed around to make room. Though he lay in the middle of a barn in the Polish countryside, he *knew* that he was back in the overcrowded prisoner transport. And he had to escape—try to flee. Standing, he thrust his way through the thickened and diseased air of the cattle car and hurled himself through the sliding door and onto the hay-covered ground, which was swirling and rushing by his feet. He landed with a grunt and looked around. He'd made it out! But somehow he had landed in what looked like a pool of vomit mixed with putrid blood and pus. But whose? And here? In the middle of the countryside? It had to be from some animal.

Éric pushed himself upwards, but for some reason his left arm didn't respond to his brain's commands. It flopped around lifeless at his side—a dead weight that scraped senseless across the ground. Why? Perhaps it was asleep. With his functioning hand, Éric placed his fingertips into the blood. It was still warm. Whatever had bled here was not far.

He looked up and scanned the landscape for clues. Nothing. No footsteps. No animal snorts or groans. No people. No prisoners. No Germans. Nothing. Just he and time ticking away as his contact was no doubt waiting at their agreed meeting spot back in France: Saint Jean Square in the old part of Lyon. At a table in the Café de Gerland. Éric was supposed to show up, order a coffee, and cross his legs while looking out over the town square. Then, and only then, would his contact approach him with the secret code, the first three lines of one of the French poet Paul Verlaine's most famous poems: "*Les sanglots longs / Des violons / De l'automne.*" *The long sobs of autumn's violins.* Then Éric would be sure that his contact was authentic, and not some goddamned German spy or some French collaborationist asshole trying to trick him into revealing his identity. No, they had their code. And he was confident he would not be found out. No, he'd already learned his lesson once. His foolishness had already gotten him arrested and into the police and

Gestapo registry. And to think *his* father had been the one to turn him in after everything! No, he had gotten everything right this time. Planned everything. Everything.

Except his package! Where had he left it?

Pushing himself up to a tottering standing position, Éric swiveled his head around aimlessly, looking, looking, looking. His eyes had become milky and glazed in his delirium, and bright red blood oozed from his left shoulder as he tottered around the empty storage barn. Like one possessed, he pounced at the first stack of hay that he saw and flipped it over with his right hand, plunging his head around the bundle as it rolled, as if expecting some small but speedy rodent to flee at the sight of day. Nothing. He lunged again and again at the hay, pulling, tugging, yanking, tumbling. He knocked over stacks, meter high, but stopped short of trying to dislodge the larger pieces. In a few minutes, he had transformed a corner of the barn into an unruly mess of hay bales that looked like some child's blocks that had been tossed about.

Out of breath and faint, Éric stopped in the middle of the pile and whirled about. Sweat drenched his ashen features, and the tendons and muscles in his neck bulged through his sunken skin like small cords pulled to their breaking point. His eyes lolled around in his sockets, focusing on nothing in particular and everything at once. He stumbled forward, paused, took two more steps, and emerged onto the edge of the frozen barley field that stretched out from the barn and towards the wood about a kilometer away. He placed his hand on one of the wooden barn supports to steady himself and looked off to the left. There, about a hundred yards away was a lone road that stretched along the length of the field before curving off left and disappearing over a small crest.

"*Voilà!*" Éric gasped as he staggered toward the road. This road must lead to the old part of Lyon. If he could just make it there and keep walking, he'd be sure to arrive in time. But what time was it? The sky glowed a dismal gray that revealed neither morning nor evening. Maybe noon? No matter. Step, step, step, step, step.

As he walked, a soft tune floated over the wood and across the fields, tickling Éric's ears. He paused and looked around. No one. He listened, his ears straining over the pounding of his heart and the wheezing of his breath. There it was again—there was no doubt. It was "La Marseillaise," the French national anthem. Someone was humming his country's national anthem! It must mean something! He *would* live!

Feeling a warmth and pride that he'd last felt with his mother before she'd died so many years ago, Éric stood tall and continued walking. As the humming bled into words, a faint smile crossed his chapped lips.

Allons, enfants de la patrie, le jour de gloire est arrivé !

Come on, children of the nation, the day of glory has arrived !

The voice was clear and in perfect tune, and resonated through Éric's battered and atrophied body. The words gave him strength—strength to defy anything the Nazis could ever do to him, to his country, to his friends, to Europe, to the Jews. The words were true, noble, and pure.

Contre nous de la tyrannie, l'étendard sanglant est levé,

Entendez-vous dans nos campagnes mûgir les féroces soldats?

Down with tyranny, the bloody flag is raised,

Do you hear the ferocious soldiers roaring in our fields?

Éric's feet reached the cold asphalt, his wooden prisoner's clogs clunking their way across the surface. His entire body trembled—from fatigue, from effort, from the overwhelming mirage that engulfed him. Since his escape, this was the most he'd exerted himself beyond lifting food to his mouth. Coupled with the loss of blood and the fatal infection that coursed through his veins, the toll of his ordeal was tragic. His mind swam with visions from his childhood, mingled with images of his friends from Lyon: Antoine, Sylvie. Mirage-like images belched forth: from his arrest by the French police and interrogation and torture by the Gestapo, to flashbacks of his days spent cramped in a cattle car lumbering across Europe with hundreds of other prisoners bound for the Hell on Earth which was *Konzentrationslager* Himmelweg, the Path to Heaven.

Ils viennent jusque dans nos bras égorger nos fils et nos compagnes.

Aux armes, les citoyens! Formez vos bataillons!

Marchons, marchons, qu'un sang impur abreuve nos sillons!

They're coming into our arms to slit our sons' and comrades' throats.

Get your arms, citizens! Form your battalions!

Let's march, march, and may an unclean blood water our fields!

Later, when the German patrol that found Éric delivered their report, it was met with laughter and disbelief.

"*Bitte*? I'm sorry? You say that you found this prisoner staggering in the middle of the road in the middle of the country? In broad daylight?"

"*Jawohl*, Hauptscharführer Heuchler!"

"And what did you say he was doing?"

"Singing, Hauptscharführer!"

"Singing?"

"*Jawohl!*"

"And what was he singing, if I may ask?"

"I am not sure, Hauptscharführer. It was in French."

"In French?"

"*Jawohl*, Hauptscharführer! I could not understand, but I think the escaped prisoner was singing France's national anthem."

"The national anthem? So a prisoner who'd just escaped from the *Konzentrationslager* was wandering down a road in Poland in the middle of winter, still in his prisoner's clothing. Near death, you say? And singing, or didn't you say nearly screaming, the French national anthem?"

"*Jawohl*, Herr Hauptscharführer Heuchler!"

"I see. And what happened next?"

ДЕСЯТЬ
TEN

JULIA OPENED HER EYES AND LOOKED AROUND. THE CRYPT
glowed in the light of the four candles that Father
Witold had kept lit since she arrived. The meager
flames provided a modicum of warmth in the stone-
walled room. Still, Julia kept herself tucked far
underneath the covers to fight off the cold.

For the first time since she'd arrived, she felt
the strength to sit up and move around. A lancing
pain still rocketed through her back as she shifted
her position, but Witold's daily helpings of broth
had helped her to put back at least a little of the
much-needed weight. Now, when she ran her hands
across her chest, her ribs no longer pushed through

the skin like a cage enclosing some small, thumping animal. She still needed a doctor—there was no question about that. But right now her main priority was just to survive—to survive here in hiding, away from the Gestapo and the war. She wondered how far away the Americans and Soviets were. Matthiew had said they were close. But how close was close? Days? Weeks? Months?

Easing her legs over the edge of her improvised bed, Julia lowered her socked feet to the floor. Even through the wool covering her soles, the stone's cold chilled her feet and legs. At least she could feel the difference in temperature now. When she'd first come in, she'd lost all feeling in her feet and hands.

Putting her weight on her feet, she stood. When she did not tumble over, she let out an audible chuckle—her first since her arrest.

"Feeling better?" Witold's voice surprised her from behind. Julia had not heard the priest descend the steps from the nave above to the crypt. She turned and smiled, letting out a long sigh. The cross around Witold's neck shone in the candlelight.

"Yes. I think I might even be able to walk."

"Let's see." Witold took two steps toward her, his arms held out from his sides in case she were to stumble.

Like a toddler taking her first steps, Julia put one foot in front of the other, slowly rolling the balls of her feet around and over the stone floor before easing her full weight onto each foot. At first, she swung her trailing foot forward in anticipation of a fall. But with each step she gained confidence and took her time more and more, as if savoring this new freedom. With Father Witold in the middle of the room, she made her way around the small crypt's perimeter, walking alongside the walls and looking at every corner of the somber room for the first time. As she walked, she paused and flexed her legs before standing tall and stretching on her toes. She smiled once more and turned to Witold, who had sat down on the edge of her bed. He was no longer watching her. Instead, he was gazing at the floor with vacant eyes. Sadness covered his face. Julia paused, her eyes riveted on the man she'd known since her childhood. Ever since her father had . . .

"Father?" her voice broke the silence. Witold made no reply. "Father, what is it?" She walked over and sat on the bed next to him. The old priest looked up. As he did, Julia's eyes fell on the cross hanging around his neck.

"Julia," he began, turning his gaze on her. His bright blue eyes had grown cloudy.

"Yes, father?"

"There is a problem. A big one. *I* have a problem. One that I have tried to take care of on my own. But I can see no other way now."

"Yes?"

Witold sighed deeply and stood. Now he paced the room, his hands clasping each other behind his back. As he strode around the crypt, he avoided her eyes. Instead he kept his gaze fixed on one of the candles, whose flame flitted about in what seemed to be a feeble draft that was trickling down from above.

"These are hard times," he continued as the flame danced. Behind him, his twisted shadow writhed about on the stone wall like some specter or demon. "It has always been my goal to help you. You know this. I brought you in from your . . . from your father. And now, I've more than happily given you the food from my table.

"But now, my child, I have no more food. I can afford no more. There is nothing. Not even for me. You must go. You must. Before . . . "

Julia stared blankly. Her mouth dropped open.

"Before what?" she asked.

Witold paused. He looked at one of the candles, whose light flickered out as the wick disappeared into a puddle of molten wax. He turned and faced her.

"There is one chance," he said. He stepped towards her bed. His eyes glowed in the remaining light, as if lit from within by some strange fire. "I need money. There is *nothing*. But you . . . your house." He nodded in the direction of Gustaw's house. "Your . . . your godfather had money. He'd told me about this. Hidden." Witold now looked intently at Julia. "You must . . . you must get it— the money," he said, his voice solid and clear. "You must go to your house. There *must* be something there. Surely? You know the house better than I. You lived there for years. And it is right next door," he pointed, as if Julia didn't know and needed a reminder. This is the only way I might be able to keep you here for a few more days, until Matthiew can get you out. Elsewhere. But without money, I might be forced to act sooner."

A wave of adrenaline coursed through Julia. Her heart beat faster and ice chilled the base of her neck. Her thoughts flew to the space underneath the flat stone to the left of the downstairs fireplace, where she'd hidden her savings since moving in with Gustaw so many years ago. But the Germans, the ones living in her house: what about them? What if they had found the money? And why her? But more than the thought of trying to rob her own house, she was terrified that the village priest—the man who'd heard her confessions so many times and even who'd baptized her—was now threatening her.

"But why?" she asked meekly. "Father, I've known you for so long. Father, what did they say to you? Why did the Germans . . . "

"Here, there are no whys, I'm afraid," Witold interrupted, holding his hand up to stop her. "Times are hard. There is nothing. *Nothing*. I am receiving pressure, much pressure. From others. From the other villagers. From . . . the Germans. If only you knew . . . So if you cannot find anything, you must—" He averted his eyes.

"Must what?" Julia's voice trembled.

Witold looked back at the candle and crossed himself. In the low light, his lips quivered. He mumbled to himself and turned his back on her. "I will bring you some new clothes," he said, walking toward the stairway. "You must find money soon. Or else," a muffled sob caught in his throat. "Or else I must release you into *God's* hands. And the village—and I'm sure, the Germans—would surely be stunned to find out that you are a *Jew*."

A flash flew before Julia's eyes as her fear boiled into rage. She shook her head in disbelief at what she'd just heard. What happened to the Witold she'd known since childhood? Who had he been speaking to? Why this sudden change?

"A *Jew*?" she snapped, her lip quivering. "What are you talking about? I'm Catholic, and even that only because . . . Why?" she stepped toward the priest and clamped her hand on his shoulder, spinning him around. As he turned, he reached up and grabbed her hand, squeezing until her joints cracked. Julia winced as Witold leaned in to within inches of her face. The reek of stale vodka wafted from his breath. In the span of just seconds, he'd transformed from an angel to a devil—one she'd never seen or known, but one that terrified her to the core. What did the priest know that he wasn't telling her?

"Just get the goddamned money," he hissed, releasing her hand. "There's no other way. I've tried everything else." And without another word, he stumbled from the room.

Father Witold disappeared after that morning. Before, Julia could tell that he was upstairs. A scrape or scuffle would echo through the nave, a door would close, or the floorboards would creak. But since ordering Julia to break into her own house, Witold had let the church fall into a deep, silent slumber—its transept and sacristy chilled with the weight of the Polish winter air. Julia knew he'd be back, though. At the entrance to the crypt he'd left a pile of thick winter clothes and worn-but-sturdy boots as an invitation for her to make good on his wish.

Julia stepped over the pile and lifted the corduroy pants, turning the rough cloth in her hands. Should she run away? Escape? Again? Escape from her rescuer? Since Witold's order, she felt she could no longer believe in the man that had always been so kind to her. Her mind spun through the village's inhabitants, in search of someone she could trust to feed and hide her both from the Germans and now, Father Witold. With each person that came to mind there also came the realization that she didn't know if the people were even alive or still in the village. But even if they were, she'd be asking them to defy the village priest—someone who'd held sway over the inhabitants of Piekło for at least two decades.

No, she decided, there was too much uncertainty. And besides, she was in no physical shape to run from anyone who might challenge her. Father Witold had cared for her for at least several weeks—time when she easily could have been discovered, but she hadn't. Surely he was just acting in desperation. But robbing a family of Germans? Even if they may have been living in her house? It was suicide. But refusing to go? Would Witold make good on his threat?

Over the next two days, Julia crept up from her makeshift bedroom both day and night and tucked herself away near the window of the sacristy, where she could peek out at the village. From her vantage point, she could observe the road and Gustaw's house, which lay some one hundred meters down the street from the church. How many times as a child and teenager had she walked the short distance between the two buildings to go to mass or confession? She could make the trip blindfolded. But now . . . now she was faced with walking the other direction. And for very different reasons.

Every time she looked out, the house was empty and dark. Or at least it seemed so. During the day the wooden shutters remained closed and latched, and at night the house was little more than a black, angular silhouette against a starry blue-black sky. Had Witold been right about there being a German family in the house? Or had he just been spreading rumors? For even if the Germans had acquisitioned the house, they appeared to be elsewhere.

And then a thought—a spark of hope—shot through Julia's mind: What if the German family had been reacting to the news of the Americans' and Soviets' advance? What if they had fled? The more she thought about it, the more the possibility seemed probable, even likely. After all, it was doubtful that the family would've gone away on some sort of vacation—not now, not during the darkest hours of the war. And especially not when the Americans and the Soviets were closing in.

No, that had to be it. They had to have fled. There was no other explanation.

On the third night of her watch, Julia donned the clothes left by Father Witold. She pulled on the pants and the chemise and noticed that these were men's clothes both by their cut and by their size— they drooped around her waist and hung low from her shoulders. Witold had left a short rope that Julia threaded through the belt buckles and pulled tight, knotting the ends in front of her waist. The top of the pants now pinched together uncomfortably. She pulled on the boots and jacket and slid once more to the sacristy window.

Her blood froze at what she saw.

Several hundred meters away, past Gustaw's house and near the intersection of the village's two roads, a black Mercedes convertible turned in her direction and accelerated, its cloth top fastened tight to the windshield. A German car. In the years leading up to her imprisonment, and during her time in KL Himmelweg, she'd seen Nazis and Gestapo using precisely this type of car. More often than not it would be followed by a green military truck with soldiers and gear. But now there was just this one car.

It was heading toward the church.

Her pulse quickening, Julia stepped back from the window of the sacristy. She spun her head around as if expecting Matthiew to be behind her. But the room was empty. Her breath came in short, rapid bursts, and her flesh crept with terror. She tried to steady her panting and listen, her eyes squinting through the window at the piercing white headlights that drew closer, closer, and closer like the eyes of some approaching devil. Julia held her breath. Surely the car would just speed past, as she'd seen so many do since the war had begun.

With a sputtering of flying gravel and a squeal of brakes that needed lubricating, the Mercedes veered from the road and skidded to a stop in front of the church.

Julia panicked. Fighting back tears of terror, she spun around and flew through the sacristy door, a white-hot pain lancing her side with every step. The oversized men's pants rustled and fought against her frail legs as she slid across the church's nave to the crypt door. She flung it open and threw herself inside. Just as she yanked the door shut, the sound of its latching was echoed through the building by the clangor of the church's front doors being thrown open and several men's voices shouting back and forth to each other.

They were shouting in German.

With trembling and sweaty hands, Julia fumbled to turn the massive skeleton key in the crypt's lock, locking herself in with the dead. She wrenched the key out with a metallic scrape and let it clank its way down the marble stairs below. Sobs racked her still weak body as she slid down the stairs and into the room where she'd spent the past few weeks convalescing. For the first time since Witold had taken her in, she noticed a familiar but horrifying smell that she'd smelled only once before: in KL Himmelweg. It was the smell she'd encountered while working with the *Sonderkommando* and tending the geese. It was the reek that wafted from the gas chambers each time the S.S. opened them up after a group of prisoners had been "processed." It was the odor of hundreds of bodies piled on top of each other just before they'd be dragged out and incinerated in the camp's crematoria. It was the aroma of Death.

Julia scurried into the murky crypt. The candles were out but she'd spent so much time here she could move around blind. With her hands outstretched, she slipped over to her improvised bed and crouched down behind it like a child playing hide-and-seek. Above the room, the Germans had made it to the locked door, which rattled in its frame as they hurled their bodies against it. Once. Twice. Four times. Julia could hear the Germans swearing as they struggled with the door. When a thought chilled her veins.

How did they know to head straight for the crypt? The church was much larger than that, with plenty of other places to hide.

For that matter, how did they know to come to the church?

Someone had betrayed her.

But who?

A pause in the banging from above. A pause that gave Julia her answer. A new, softer voice said something, quieting the Germans. A voice she recognized.

Witold's voice.

There was a jangle from above, followed by the rattle of a key being slid into the keyhole. The crypt's key. Hers was not the only one.

The key turned.

The door swung open with a creak.

"NOOOOOOOOO!" Julia's hysterical voice exploded through the stone room and echoed through the church above. Her shredding vocal cords stunned her into a catatonic stupor and she crumpled onto the floor in a heap. Her body twitched and curled in on itself as she clutched her knees to her chest and began to rock back and forth, humming to herself.

White circles of light danced down the staircase and around the room. Heavy, booted steps reverberated through the crypt.

"*Die haben wir ja.*"

"*Jawohl.*"

"*Das wird ja dem Strauss gefallen.*"

The German voices rained down into the room like slivers of icy hail slicing through Julia's heart.

The steps came closer.

Light shone in Julia's eyes from her place on the floor. She looked up into four glaring suns that burned down on her. There was a pause. She gazed into the light and the Germans contemplated her, as if trying to decide for a moment what to do.

The suns parted and one of the men stepped forward and crouched beside Julia.

A hand gripped her shoulder.

As the lights moved aside, she glimpsed the German's face.

Stockhausen. The Gestapo officer who'd originally searched her farm and unearthed the buried memories of her father. The man who'd first driven her to try and help those poor souls on the transports. Who'd pushed her to her arrest. Who'd caused her to end up in KL Himmelweg in the first place.

"We meet again, *Fräulein*."

Julia screamed. Again and again and again and again.

"NOOOOOOOOOO!" she shrieked, every vein and tendon in her neck and head straining at the effort. Her scream was something inhuman—something that had belched forth from the depths of Hell. Before her breath had even faltered, tears streamed down her cheeks and spit dripped from the corners of her mouth. She screamed again. She wailed. She howled.

Not since Gustaw had locked her in her room nearly two years before had the depths of Julia's suffering ripped through Piekło in such an agonizing swan song—one that resonated throughout the village.

As she wailed, Stockhausen's chiseled Aryan features twisted into an evil smirk. In the light from the flashlights Julia saw that three soldiers stood behind him. Each dressed in drab green Wehrmacht uniforms, they clutched submachine guns across their chests and cast a bovine gaze on their victim, who had slumped down onto her back, her head smacking dully against the ceramic tile floor.

"WHYWHYWHYWHYWHY?" Julia wailed like a wounded animal, ramming her head with increasing force against the floor. *Whump, whump, whump, whump.* Her arms and legs thrashed about, knocking into the wall, her bed, the floor. Seeing the violence with which she was butting her head into the stone floor, Stockhausen lunged forward and latched his hand around her ankle. With a superhuman tug, he launched her into the middle of the crypt, where she slid to a stop in between the four men. Without pausing, Stockhausen lifted his polished, knee-high boot and sent it crushing down onto Julia's right arm. With a howl of pain, she reached over with her free hand and clawed at the Nazi's boot. But it was planted firmly in place. Stockhausen leaned over to thrust the barrel of his pistol under her chin and pushed her head backwards, pinning her against the floor. Julia's thrashing subsided, and her shrieks faded into heart-wrenching whimpers as her will to live faded.

"Listen to me, you bitch," Stockhausen spat, his face inches from Julia's. "We have you now. *Again*." He chuckled and looked as his men, who continued to stare stupidly at the scene unfolding in front of them. They'd seen this all before. Work was work, and it was late. Their minds already longed for their shift to end. Perhaps they'd have a drink together before they went home, or if they were lucky, a Polish woman who'd consent to be with them for the night in exchange for protection.

"Give the priest his money," Stockhausen turned and said to one of the soldiers.

"*Jawohl*," the man barked, turning and walking back up the stairs.

Julia's eyes lolled into her skull as the suffocating truth settled in.

The next few minutes might have been a dream. Or they might have been reality. As the Germans' ogre-like hands reached down to grab Julia's arms and legs, hoisting her up and carrying her up the stairs, she had the impression of flying. But not merely gliding over the stone floor of the crypt, she felt as though she were flying high, high above Piekło, above the clouds even, and gazing down at the village below as angels carried her up, up, up and toward Heaven. She rose above the village where she'd grown up and had been so badly hurt along with her brother, been taken in by Gustaw, moved past the trauma of her childhood, become a strong young woman, fought against the Nazis' terror by trying to bring some semblance of succor to the condemned as they languished on their way to certain death, and now, now, where she'd been betrayed by the only man she thought she could trust. A man who stood at the top of the crypt stairs and gazed at her with moistened and sad eyes as the Germans carried her limp body past, through the nave, and out the door of Piekło's only church.

With soft, inaudible footsteps, Witold followed the men through the edifice, pausing at the main doorway. A hand on his shoulder startled him. He turned. It was Stockhausen.

"Thank you for your support of the Reich," he said, distracted. "We may need your help again in the days and weeks to come."

Witold didn't answer. With a final nod, Stockhausen stepped out of the church and turned back to the priest.

"Heil Hitler," he snapped, lifting his arm in a Hitler salute and turning back to the black Mercedes. Two of the soldiers were working Julia into the back seat, while the third climbed into the driver's seat. Without looking back at the church or at Witold, Stockhausen opened the passenger door, sat in the leather seat, and slammed the door behind him.

Back in the church's doorway, Witold wiped his eyes with the back of his sleeve and watched the car's taillights burn red as the driver pressed the brakes while cranking the car. The engine roared to life, rupturing the silence that enveloped the sleepy village of Piekło. The red lights dimmed, and the car pulled out of the gravel lot and onto the paved road. The crunch and rustle of tires gave way to the smooth swish of rubber rolling over asphalt. The car's taillights swept down Piekło's main road and to the intersection beyond Gustaw's house. They flashed red as the car braked and faded with the renewed acceleration. The Mercedes turned left and headed towards Bierún.

But then something happened. About three hundred meters away from Gustaw's house, the car screeched to a halt. Because it was now more than a half kilometer away, Witold could no longer hear the motor, but he sensed that the car was sitting there in the middle of the road, idling.

The car's lights vanished into the darkness. The driver had killed the motor. Silence. Because the nighttime sky was blanketed in clouds, Witold could see neither the road nor the vehicle. But he knew the Germans were still there. Doing what? Talking? Planning? Had there been a mechanical problem?

Why did they turn off all of the car's lights just to sit in the middle of the road? Something was wrong.

Beyond the church's grounds, Piekło slept, unaware of what was happening in their midst. Houses sat dark in the night, their windows boarded with latched shutters, and lights inside hidden by blackout curtains. The roads and fields were empty, the only movement coming from the occasional winter breeze or the rapid, finger-like scratching of rats scuttling through rigid stumps of hay. No other cars. No motors.

But Piekło's dreams were fitful. For at the darkest hour of the night and the moment of her deepest sleep, the village stirred from the sound of a struggle. A car door opening. German voices swearing. A woman's voice, broken with terror or resignation—it was hard to tell.

Witold watched.

Witold listened.

The Germans had stepped out of the car and pulled Julia out with them, for their voices danced over the fields. A struggle. A scream pierced the night. Another. Scrapes of feet across the asphalt. A sentence spoken in German. A man's voice. More high-pitched screams in the night—Julia's screams.

And then silence.

A teardrop-shaped spurt of orange.

The blow of a lone gunshot echoed from the road near the church and smacked off the stucco walls of the city hall, the school, and the festival hall. Those who were awake and heard the shot said later that it must've been an accident because they'd heard only one. If it had been the Germans, they reasoned, there would've been others. At least that's what they'd been told by villagers from elsewhere: whenever the Nazis performed an *Aktion*, a roundup, they did it to the staccato tune of hundreds of small and large explosions. Still others wondered if it had been a suicide: someone who just couldn't take the suffering and unending hopelessness brought by the Germans. In the days that followed, no police came, no bodies were found, and nothing suspicious seemed to be happening. Just a lone, errant shot in the night.

But after that shot, Piekło never again heard screams in the night.

Witold's breath failed him. As the lone, black Mercedes once again roared to life across the fields, its lights speeding into the distance, the priest disappeared into the church. His head spinning, he stumbled through the nave and fell to his knees to where he knew the sculpture of the Virgin Mary stood somber against the wall, her eyes turned sadly downwards to face the suffering of the world. Witold wept, his sobs echoing through the Romanesque building. Reaching forward, he rested his right hand on the rope that formed a barrier around the antique sculpture. His hand trembled, shaking the rope in its supports, jostling the silence. Outside, the wind howled. A winter storm approached.

Five days later, Piekło suffered a horrifying shock when it was time for mass. One more to add to their litany of pains brought on by the German terror.

Discovered by the first churchgoers on a warmer Sunday morning, Father Witold's body dangled silently from a frayed rope attached to a rafter in the nave's ceiling. His skin had become pasty and yellow, and his swollen tongue bulged unnaturally from his mouth. Off to the side of the nave, the statue of the Virgin lay smashed in a thousand pieces upon the stone floor.

The priest had hanged himself.

ОДИННАДЦАТЬ
ELEVEN

"**Y**OU MUST GO."

The raspy Polish words stirred Russ from the deepest sleep he'd had in years. Despite the straw ticking poking his body and the fleas and bedbugs gnawing and creeping over his flesh, the warmth of his bed and the fullness of his stomach lured him back to sleep. Was it a dream? Bodily sensations faded as his mind numbed again.

"Now!" His mattress shook as someone thrust their full body weight into it.

In a fit of panic, Russ jerked awake and sat up, his hands darting about for his rifle, which he'd left at his side. He relaxed when he saw the old woman leaning over his bed. And then he remembered: the cold, the sausage, the fire, the brandy, the civilian clothes. He tried to muster a smile. Behind the woman, Józef was already up, dressed, and pulling a pair of suspenders over his shoulders as he spoke.

"The sun will be up in an hour," he said. The old woman stood and shuffled out of the room. "The Bug River's not far. We should cross before light."

Russ nodded and threw his legs onto the floor, standing. Józef bowed to a pile of clothes that the woman had placed on the foot of his bed. Russ pulled on the trousers and shirt, marveling at how close the size was to his own. A pang of regret shot through him, because he knew the woman's husband had to die for him to be able to wear this costume now. Still, he also knew that she was proud to help them in any way she could. This was her way of fighting back. *It's a shame there aren't more like her,* Russ thought as he worked his feet into the leather work boots. *Maybe then the Germans wouldn't have had such an easy time overrunning this place.*

But then he remembered the partisans that had originally found him after his plane had crashed two years ago. Maybe more people than he thought were helping, after all. Maybe the Poles—and the French, and the Dutch, and the Italians, and the Belgians, and the Czechoslovakians . . . maybe a current of resistance *did* exist under the still waters of collaboration.

He shook his head and walked out the door, his feet clumping hollowly on the wooden floor. Maybe he'd never know.

After saying good-bye to the woman and thanking her, the two men set out eastward into the pre-dawn gloom. At this hour, the only people they risked seeing were German patrols as the city was still under curfew. Knowing this, they avoided Zeberka's roads and buildings, winding their way circuitously through fields, ditches, and empty lots. Every few steps, Russ searched the sky for the North Star, which he kept to his left. Aside from the crunch of their freshly shod feet in the frozen snowpack, no sounds escaped the men—no words, no grunts, no noisy breaths. If they had to communicate, Russ would stop and turn around, reaching out through the dark until Józef met his hand. Then, with only the sliver of moon as their light, he would gesture, pointing out any fences, holes, carts, or trash bins that might be blocking their way. Not that Russ was worried that the two could injure themselves. But they couldn't afford to make any noise, especially the noise of a nighttime prowler stumbling over some unseen obstacle. If anything would attract the Germans, that would.

Because they were feeling their way through the night, and because they were weaving in and around yards, fields, and hedges, a walk that would've taken ten minutes by road took nearly forty-five. Off in the east, the sky was beginning to lose its darkness to the coming sun, and it was the sun's timid glow that announced their arrival at the river. For there, in the middle of the black expanse of a barley field, the calm, silver trail of a sluggish waterway snaked its way toward the North Sea.

The Bug River.

On this side, German-occupied Poland, on the other, Stalin's Red Army, which was creeping westward in the Ukraine, a force so powerful that possibly only a fool would challenge them. Hitler had done so four years before before by violating the von Ribbentrop Non-Aggression Pact and invading the Soviet Union.

When Russ and Józef reached the western bank, they paused and looked up and downstream. In the growing light, their breaths puffed visibly in the cold.

"Now we must cross," Józef whispered. Russ nodded.

"Even if there were a bridge here," the Pole continued, squatting and peering as far as he could downstream, "that would not be possible. Hm. It would be guarded.

"Swim across?"

"No choice."

"And the cold?"

Józef thought at Russ's question. He ran his right hand across the front of his new clothes. A shiver stirred his limbs.

"We must take off our clothes," he said, reaching for the buttons below his collar. "We shall die of cold if we swim with these on. We must try to dry on other side and then put on clothes that are not wet." In one movement, he yanked his shirt from his shoulders and tossed it over his shoulder. He began unbuckling his belt. "Can you swim?"

"Yes," Russ answered, pulling the suspenders from his shoulders. "God be with us."

"Hmm."

The two men shed layer after layer of clothing in silence. Their hands and arms shook more and more violently, making it difficult for them to work their fingers around buttons and buckles. The frigid air latched onto their skin, sucking the warmth from their body, and the snow lanced their bare feet with the excruciating needles of frostbite. Their breaths tumbled out in short, rapid, staccato bursts, as their diaphragms were torn with spasms.

A passerby stumbling upon the scene would've been horrified by the skeletal specters dancing about naked in the snow. Though both men were tall, their bones protruded from shrunken and ashen skin pulled tight. Most pronounced of all were the two men's pelvises, which jutted out like some sort of morbid bowl from which dangled two gangly, bony legs. Their knees appeared as rough balls underneath their skin, and the men's ribs swelled out with each breath, threatening to rip through the skin like some ogre's massive fingers tearing apart its victim.

Russ and Józef took no notice of the other's body. In their years in the camp, emaciated and atrophied shells of human beings had become the norm. More unnatural to them now was the sight of someone well fed. For the only well-fed people they knew were Germans, and it was the Germans who had reduced them to this ghastly state. Their thoughts were solely on moving quickly enough not to succumb to the cold, but carefully enough not to make noise and attract attention.

Naked, the two men squatted in the snow and clumsily folded their clothes and shoes into a compact package, which they tied together with their shirtsleeves and the lengths of rope they'd been using as belts. With his bundle wrapped, Russ wedged the rifle through the tightly bound knot until he'd pushed it halfway through. His clothes now clung to the center of the weapon's stock, which he gripped on either side and hoisted over his head. He stepped down toward the water. Józef lifted his bundle and followed.

Despite the searing, razor-sharp pain rocketing into his calves and thighs through the soles of his bare feet, Russ paused at the river's edge and looked down. Over the course of the winter, three meters of water from the bank had frozen solid, becoming moving water farther out. Looking one last time up and downstream, he steadied the rifle over his head and eased his foot out onto the frozen surface.

The moment the flesh of his heel settled, it stuck. As he rolled his foot down fully, the calloused skin of his feet crackled and tugged as it snapped and ripped to free itself from the ice. Because he'd lost all sensation from his knees down, the minute lacerations caused no pain. But like a dentist's patient feeling the numb pressure and wiggling of teeth being pulled from his jaw, he grimaced and avoided looking down to see just how badly the ice was wounding his feet as he stepped across. He could tell that the ice was thinning the farther he stepped out. Behind him, it groaned under Józef's weight. Neither man stopped moving forward. Instead, Russ altered his walk to more of a waddle, lowering his pale, bare rear to within inches of the ice. He still held his arms high above his head, and his entire frame now bobbed and ducked. He inched his way to the water.

He paused. He looked down. In front of him, the Bug's sluggish current lapped over the edge of the ice. It was time. Emptying his lungs of air with an audible *shoosh*, Russ filled them again to bursting, his ribs cracking against his chest bone as his torso expanded. He paused once more, holding his burning breath.

And then, amid the crunching of snapping and splattering ice, he slid forward and into the water.

As his head plunged into the river, Russ was able to kick hard enough to keep his forearms and hands above water. But the power of the cold, wet mass that snapped in around him stunned all of his senses and knocked every gulp of air from his lungs. A million knives, nails, and spikes dug into his flesh, scraping and tearing away at his already numbed and worn body. It was as if in one blast, all of his skin had been ripped away, leaving nothing but exposed muscles and viscera to be frozen by the glacial Bug River. Amid the asphyxiating force of the water, he somehow managed to fight back with a guttural howl as he kicked against the current, which fortunately was slow enough at this part of the Bug not to compound their ordeal. Struggling to keep his chin and mouth above water, and feeling his arms sear from the effort of holding them straight up with a nearly ten-kilo load between them, Russ kicked and kicked and kicked and kicked and kicked and kicked. He swam, keeping his eyes fixed on one lone star straight overhead whose flame was fading with the rising sun. With every burst of shallow breath, the star disappeared behind a thick cloud of vapor, only to reappear an instant later even dimmer than before. Russ imagined that the star was counting down his time alive, and he now had to make it to the opposite shore before the star vanished into the morning light.

The ice sheet cut into his chest before his feet ever touched the bottom. Razor-thin at first, it thickened quickly, just as it had done on the western bank. Still beating against the river with his feet, Russ brought the rifle butt down with a crack, shattering the thinner ice again and again, until he'd carved out a jagged, U-shaped divot extending shoreward and into the thicker ice. Only when the rifle butt rebounded with a metallic yet tooth-numbing crunch did he fling the weapon and his bundled clothes onto the floe. They slid to a stop just as the frozen grass from the Ukrainian side was emerging from the ice. Placing his hands on either side of the hole, Russ grunted and pushed down, his elbows trembling from the effort. His body lifted up to his mid-back and then dropped back down into the water, which lapped over his shoulders and into the stubble on his shorn scalp.

"Hurry!" Józef's wavering voice shouted from behind.

With another grunt and wobbly heave, Russ pulled his now red, glistening body from the water and planted his feet on the ice. But rather than run up onto the bank, he turned and offered his hand to Józef, whose face had become pasty and his lips, blue. The Pole took the American's hand. The two squeezed each other's forearms and Russ leaned back and pulled, lifting Józef up and onto the ice.

The two hopped onto the bank, with Russ

snatching up his clothes bundle as they passed. Over the frozen hay and roots, the men climbed the shallow bank leading down to the river and disappeared over the crest at the top. Lifting their knees as high as their rigid muscles would allow, they kept running until they reached a small thicket of trees about twenty meters away from the water.

Hidden from the surrounding farmland, Russ and Józef fought a losing battle against the cold as they fumbled to rip apart their clothing bundles. Unable to grasp anything with his fingers, Russ flailed about, sending his clothes flying into a scattered mess on the ground. Before bending down, he rubbed his hands violently across his entire body in an attempt to scatter as much water from his flesh as possible before getting dressed. He shook his arms, his hands, his legs, his feet. He jumped in place in small, rapid bounds, trying in vain to flex his toes and revive them. He bent over and reached for his pants with blue, claw-like fingers. To his right, Józef was already thrusting his arms into his shirt.

"*PRIVAL!*" a voice spat at them in Russian from behind. Russ snapped up and whirled around, and Józef lowered his arms in front of his waist, his shirt stretched between his arms like a cloth blind covering his groin. Russ had not been so lucky. He stood pale and fully naked before the men who now faced them.

The Soviets.

About twenty soldiers had crept up on Russ and Józef as they had been scrabbling with their clothes in a frozen daze. The two men had heard nothing, but now they stared with icy eyes at nearly two dozen rifles pointed at their exposed bodies. Behind the weapons, soldiers in their early twenties stood tense, their jaws twitching in the cold and their fingers caressing their triggers. On each man's camouflage hat beamed a crimson star.

The Red Army.

Stalin's men.

Throwing a glance at the rifle that lay three meters away and then at Józef, Russ eased his shaking hands into the air. Józef did likewise. Both men, naked, now stared at their Russian captors.

From behind the line of soldiers, an older man gripping a pistol pushed his way through, spitting Russian sentences. He stomped toward the American and the Pole. The man, who appeared to be in his forties, was some sort of officer: a wide, circular officer's cap sat atop his fleshy ears, and a volley of glistening medals danced over the left breast of his uniform. He seemed dressed for a parade and not for a patrol just outside of German-occupied territory.

As the officer spoke, Russ never took his eyes off him. The man seemed both angry and surprised—as if this sight were more traumatic and shocking to him than any of the other horrors of the war that he may have already seen. He almost seemed as if he were trying to convince himself that these two freezing, emaciated men were real.

When the officer spoke, Józef answered in Russian. Russ glanced over to the Pole, who seemed to be explaining what Russ and Józef were doing in this condition in the middle of the winter. As he spoke, the officer scanned their two gaunt bodies. He seemed to be forming a picture in his mind of the story that Józef was now hotly recounting, his hands flying about and pointing behind them. Amid the flowing Russian sentences, of which Russ knew not a word, the word *Himmelweg* barked out two or three times. Józef had to be explaining how the two had come to escape the death camp.

When Józef had finished his explanation, an awkward and painful pause settled on the group. On one side, two skinny, naked men chattered and rattled audibly as their bodies shut down from the cold. On the other, a platoon of fully armed Russians stared them down, no doubt wondering what to do. Prepare to fight? Shoot them? Laugh? Rugged and implacable, the officer continued to glare at the two, trying to decide what to do.

He uttered a brief sentence that sounded like two words.

"He wants us to get dressed," Józef translated, bending over for his clothes. The two men quickly dressed and, once covered, they hugged their own bodies tightly and rubbed frantically, trying to bring some warmth back to their fading members.

The officer spoke again, raising his free arm and pointing to a clear spot of ground to the men's right. He stared Józef in the eye. Russ looked back and forth at the two as they exchanged words.

What little color had been left in Józef's face vanished at the officer's words. With a panicked expression, the Pole shot a glance to Russ and began chattering in Russian. His voice had a new tone—one of pleading, of terror. He waved his hands together in front of his chest frantically as if to ward off an errant driver about to run him down.

"*Nyet, nyet, nyet!*" Józef screamed, his movements becoming more and more frantic. What the hell was going on? Russ felt a surge of dread in his chest as he sensed what was about to happen. In front of him, the officer's face became crimson, and in one move he lunged forward and snatched Józef by the collar, hurling him to the ground. No sooner had Józef landed on his hands and knees than the officer grabbed Russ as well. But instead of throwing him down as he had Józef, the officer lifted his right hand and brought the metal handle of his pistol down squarely above Russ's left eye. Warm blood flowed over the American's face as another blow caught him at the base of the skull, sending spots flashing through his blurred vision and the frozen ground up to meet him.

Pushing himself up from the ground, Russ could hear Józef off to his right.

He was weeping.

They were about to die.

After all this. After the plane crash. After fighting with the partisans. After the capture, the misery, the penury, the planning, the stealing weapons, the escape. After all they had endured, Hitler's goddamned enemies were taking them for spies or Germans or who knows what, and in their drunken

Soviet bloodlust they were about to efface everything that Russ and Józef had been fighting for the
past six years.

Allowing himself to pitch forward headfirst
into the snow, Russ covered the back of his head
with both hands. No longer trembling, he tried to
conjure up images of his wife Penny back home—
images of the black-and-white picture he'd taken
with him into his service with the Air Force. The
picture that had partly burned in the wreckage of
his plane.

He closed his eyes tight and held his breath. He'd
always been told that you never heard the shot that
did it. One moment you were there, listening and
feeling and smelling and wondering and dreaming
and living, and the next minute, nothing. Not even
sleep. Not even blackness. No white light.

Just nothing.

A voice.

A man's voice.

Not the officer's. Or Józef's.

Someone else was shouting.

Someone shouting in Russian.

The shot never came.

Above and behind him, one of the Russians had run up and was prattling away at the officer. Amid the brisk Russian, Russ recognized Józef's name several times.

How could he know his name, though? No one had asked their names. And they hadn't revealed them.

Russ eased his eyes open. The snow-crusted ground lay inches from his nose and eyes. The voices continued behind him. He turned his head and tried to peer at the officer without the officer realizing that he was turning around.

One of the ordinary soldiers had broken ranks and held his hand on the officer's shoulder. He was agitated and pointed at Józef, all the while explaining something in Russian. The officer had lowered his pistol. Russ dared to push himself from the ground and turn around.

As the soldier continued to speak, the officer stepped over to Józef and leaned over, pulling him up by the back of his shirt. Józef turned around to face the gibbering soldier. And when he saw the man, every muscle in his body relaxed. His eyes widened and his mouth fell open in stupid disbelief.

"Kazik?" Józef said, his eyes moistening as he stepped toward the soldier and extended his pale hand.

"*Ya, es s mir*, Józef!" the man answered and threw his arms around Józef's neck. Russ realized that the man was now speaking Yiddish, not Russian. And Russ grasped that the two knew each other. While Józef and Kazik embraced, the officer to their left shook his head and muttered something to the rest of his soldiers, who for the first time relaxed. Some chuckled and stepped up to pat Józef on the back. All the while, Russ observed in dumb awe, his terror fading.

"What is it?" Russ asked, raising his voice to be heard over the racket.

Józef loosed his embrace from Kazik and turned to the American. He wiped tears from his eyes as he spoke.

"You don't understand," he said, sniffing. "This is Kazik Kumiega. He and I were in the ghetto together. In Poland. We fought together. Against the Germans. He was shot during one fight. I thought he was dead." Józef paused to let his emotion find voice in free-flowing tears that streamed down his bony cheeks. "But he escaped and joined the Red Army. And they can help us—help us get out. This is truly a miracle!"

ДВЕНАДЦАТЬ
TWELVE

WHEN PAUL STEPPED OUTSIDE THAT MORNING, HE noticed that the winter chill had become a little less biting. It was late February, so there was time yet before the full thaw would hit. But it was warmer, almost unnaturally so, as if some strange force were sweeping across the countryside.

As had become his habit since Éric had arrived, Paul first stood on the threshold of the farmhouse and surveyed the fields before getting to work. But his eyes were never on the beauty of the sunrise, the sounds of the stirring birds, or the parting clouds. He was combing the landscape for any sign of a patrol or other farmers moving about. For even though his neighbors were also Poles, these were not the times to be too trusting with anyone, no matter how much they'd smiled in the past. Paul knew that the trees had eyes and the walls, ears.

Only when he was sure that he was alone did he duck back into the house, emerging seconds later with a basket laden with milk, bread, sausage, and sometimes soup. Covered with a folded cloth, the basket tugged down at his forearm as he crossed the courtyard and shuffled down the cleared path to the hay barn. Sometimes he could only come at night because others would be about. He knew that doing so was to risk being caught breaking curfew, but at least he had the excuse of still being on his property. Each time he came out, he'd tried to speak with Éric—to exchange a few words—but he didn't speak French, and Éric could say only a few simple phrases in Polish. Since the war began, Paul had lost a number of friends to the defense, the *Aktionen*, or to deportations. He saw in Éric the potential for a comrade. Éric was not too much older than he was, maybe four or five years. And both were stuck on the farm. Lately Paul had become more and more worried about his new friend, though, because Éric's fever seemed to grow each day and he was clearly losing even more weight. Had he not moved, eaten, and mumbled at Paul when the farmer brought out food, Éric could've passed for a corpse. Of course there was no question of getting a doctor. Even if Paul and his father, Rodion, could afford it, the chance of their being betrayed was far too high. And then all three of them would die.

When Paul walked to the barn that day, he froze. Something was wrong. There, in the storage area, haystacks and individual tufts of hay had been tossed about, as if someone—or some people—had ransacked everything in a hysterical search for something. On the floor, splatters of blood speckled the yellowish-green dust and Éric's foul-smelling bandage lay unwound and in tatters. Paul looked up to Éric's improvised hideout.

An empty, coffin-sized hollow in the piles of

haystacks stared back at him. Some of the blankets that had formed Éric's ticking hung down from the compartment, with half remaining stuck in the area where the Frenchman had been sleeping for the past weeks.

Éric was gone.

Feeling a wave of panic surge through him, Paul's first impulse was to shout for his father, who by now was out in the fields scrounging for any potatoes that may have escaped the harvest. But he checked himself. *Avoid attracting attention at all costs.* This had been his and Rodion's motto since the war began. Now was not the time to scream out that the prisoner he'd been illegally hiding had been found by the Nazis and taken back to the prison camp.

Paul sat the basket down into the straw and ran out of the side of the barn facing the fields and wood beyond. He lifted his flattened hand to his brow and combed the glowing horizon. About two hundred meters away, at the point where the field's rise crested before sloping down to the forest,

Rodion's silhouette bent over the tilled earth. He was reaching out with his aging arms and clawing at the dirt to check for potatoes. Finding nothing, he stepped forward one or two steps and tried again. *No*, Paul thought, *if he'd gone this way, Papa would have seen him. Unless of course he'd gotten out or been arrested much earlier, during the night, perhaps . . .*

From off in the distance on the other side of the barn, the sound of someone singing prickled his ears away from the sounds of the wind, the rustling hay, and the occasional magpie chirping after insects. He tilted his head and listened. Nothing. The wind shifted in his direction. And with it, it brought no doubt: someone—a man—was singing, over by the road leading to Zeberka. A broken voice, but one that sounded familiar.

Heart pounding, Paul ran around the corner of the barn. When he saw what was happening a hundred meters away in the road, he halted and backtracked, hiding himself behind the far corner of the building. Like a sniper peeking out to aim for his target, Paul eased the top part of his head around the corner.

In the distance, just before where the road vanished into the forest, a lone, ghostly figure stumbled around the asphalt. It looked as if the person were either struggling to keep his balance or dancing the foxtrot, keeping step with the song he was singing. Every few seconds, the man stopped in the middle of the road, planted both feet, and puffed out his chest while reaching both arms in the air like an opera singer belting out a high note. But the man wasn't singing opera. And it wasn't a performer.

It was Éric.

He was singing the French national anthem.

When Paul recognized his wandering friend, he struggled with the violent urge to rush across the field, grab his comrade by the arms, and pull him back to safety.

But some twenty meters in front of Éric, a black German Mercedes sat purring away, its gears in neutral but its motor humming, as if getting ready to take off at any moment. In front of the car and between the vehicle's grille and Éric, a Gestapo officer stood in his long, black leather trench coat, his arms motioning at his side. He seemed to be explaining something. Éric continued to sing, pausing only to leer at the German before continuing his dance of death.

The German was becoming agitated. He paced back and forth, looked back through the angled windshield and into the car, and turned to face Éric. He planted his fists squarely on his hips. He said something, his voice rumbling over the distance to Paul's hiding place. What did he say? Éric froze and stared the German down, as if challenging him to a duel like in the American westerns. But only the German had a gun.

A pause.

The running motor.

A frigid gust stung Paul's cheek from the north, letting him know that winter hadn't gone yet.

And then, letting out an inhuman roar, Éric

screamed and rushed at the German with a force Paul never could've expected from someone this malnourished, weak, and ill. Like a rugby player, Éric covered the ten meters separating the two in seconds, before the German could pull his pistol from his holster. The Nazi was fumbling with his belt as Éric jumped into the air and collided with him full force in the chest, knocking him over with one blow. Wrapping his arms around the German in a giant bear hug, Éric tumbled with the soldier to the ground in one heap. No sooner had the two collided with the asphalt than Éric pushed himself up and launched a barrage of punches and elbows to the German's face, chest, and arms. The Gestapo pulled his leather-covered arms above his face as the blows rained down again and again and again and again. It was as if Éric had never been sick or weak at all. His strength overpowered the German.

Feeling a wave of euphoria, Paul jumped out from behind the barn and ran toward Éric. He couldn't run the risk of the German's somehow wrestling Éric off and taking vengeance. He had to help. He would fight as well, no matter what the consequences. He'd had enough.

Paul had hardly taken five steps when a second soldier opened the car door and stepped out, his pistol drawn and pointed toward the two men at the front of the car.

Oh, my God. Paul dug his heels into the ground and skidded to a stop in the still-frozen dirt. His neck and head burst with the pressure of his blood coursing through his veins. He wavered, not sure to run forward, stand still, or run back.

The German stepped forward and paused, his arm straight out from his body.

The pistol aimed at Éric.

At Paul's friend.

"NOOOOOOOOOOO!" he screamed, hoping to distract the German perhaps long enough to do something. Anything. Anything but just stand there and watch. How could anyone just watch atrocities happen and do nothing? Say nothing? It was inhuman.

The Germans ignored him, as if he'd made no sound. His throat stung and his hearing rang from the effort. His head spun.

A small yellow flare spat a puff of bluish-white smoke from the pistol's muzzle. A second later,

BAMBAMBAMBAMBAMBAM!

The shot rang out over the fields and trees.

Paul fell to his knees and brought his hands to his temples.

Tears streamed down his cheeks.

There, in the middle of the frigid asphalt of the lonely road leading from Próg to Zeberka, the emaciated body of a student and French Resistance fighter lurched forward and collapsed in a heap.

THIRTEEN

"**F**IGHT BACK!"

The Russian Yvgeny had hardly opened his mouth when the wall erupted in a hailstorm of concrete, rocks, and dust. His body buckled into the rubble, a pool of blood spreading from his ears and nape. His legs twitched as if running in his sleep. His eyes, glossy, stared upwards into the swirling clouds filling the classroom. The thunder of machine gun fire shook the walls and the ceiling.

Clickclickclick.

The hammer of Russ's rifle snapped into an empty chamber. He swore, threw the weapon aside in a metallic clash, and dove for Yvgeny's Luger, which lay under a cinder block. To his left, Józef crouched over his rifle, firing, the blasting muzzle just beyond the shattered wall. The Karabin belched out searing brass cartridges that pinged onto the frozen ground. Bullets whizzed over his head and lodged themselves into the wall, throwing out ever more clouds of concrete and plaster.

Russ, dressed in a Red Army uniform, dragged himself through the growing pile of dust, and crawled over to his new comrade's side and peeked out above the broken wall. Some forty yards away, the samurai-like helmets of the Germans darted between bushes, stones, and walls. Russ heard a muzzle blast to the left, an explosion of bluish smoke to the right, and Teutonic voices swearing everywhere, *"Donnerwetter verdammt noch mal diese verfluchten Russen!" Damn these goddamned Russians!* Behind them, the smoking barrel of a lumbering Panzer lowered, adjusting its aim. A soldier clambered onto the back of the green beast and shouted something into the open hatch.

Russ leaned forward and aimed. His wrist leapt with each heartbeat, but he steadied his breath. He placed the small nib of the pistol's front sight in the middle of the soldier's torso.

BAM! BAMBAM!

The German fell like a puppet whose strings had just been cut. Blasts to the left and right. Russ aimed at the mushroom-like helmets glinting in the bushes, bushes where children had no doubt hidden and played hide-and-seek. Before the Germans had invaded. Before the war.

BAM!

Russ's bullet opened a helmet as though it were twisting flower petals. The soldier drooped. Someone from inside the now-moving tank pushed the body to the ground into a heap, where it was tangled and crushed in the tank's treads. Russ fired three more rounds before the pistol clicked empty.

"Shit!" he slumped under the window and looked over at Yvgeny's body. Three more magazines were still clipped to his belt. In a breath, he slid over on his stomach and reached out for the ammunition. Just as his fingers closed around a magazine, an ear-piercing shriek swooped in from behind, tearing over their heads and toward the German positions. Recognizing the sound, Russ buried his head into the earth and covered his neck with his arms.

Artillery. Twenty kilometers behind them, near the German-Polish border, the Red Army had received their coordinates and opened fire. And now the heavens rained down death on the Germans.

The ground shook and Russ's breath was blown from his body. The Russian shells slammed into the line of tanks thirty meters in front. Russ's ears screeched from the shock of the explosions. He heard nothing else. No screams. No tank motors. No Germans. Not even the sound of the explosions. These he sensed in his bones and lungs, which felt as though they would be rattled from his body. The artillery poured down, sending blasts of dirt and rubble raining over the Red Army soldiers. Russ wondered at how accurate the Russians were with their aim. Part of him even wondered what his life as a soldier would've been like had he grown up a Soviet, and not just tagged along as an American ally in arms.

Almost as soon as the artillery barrage had begun, it was over. An unnatural stillness fell over the battle scene, filling Russ with a numbing unease. The smell of gunpowder, lead, and burning flesh pricked his nostrils. He looked up. Bits of dirt tumbled from his neck and head, crackling as they dropped to the snow.

Quiet.

Looking off to his left, he saw Józef pushing himself up. Russ could still not get used to seeing the former prisoner in a donated Red Army uniform. Russ wondered too how he looked in his borrowed Russian clothes. Now that he'd gotten his strength back after several weeks of rations as he marched westward with the Russians, he was thankful that the Soviets had invited him and Józef to join them. "You know the Germans," they had said, "and you know fighting. You could help." Russ shook his head. During the war he'd served in the American, Polish, and Russian armies. How would his officers back home take it? Surely not as defection, since these were allies and, after all, what choice did he have?

Russ stood and looked around. A few of the Russians' bodies lay sprawled amidst the demolished houses, walls, and buildings. The name *Torgau* peeked through a splintered tree that had fallen against a house—so this is what a German village looks like. Or looked like. Aside from smoke and flames spurting up from the Germans' Panzers out front, there was no movement from the German side. The wider space just outside the village edge had become a slaughterhouse. As the Soviets had approached the city, the Germans had pulled back, turning around at the last minute to fight. The fight had been short. The German army was falling to its knees.

The line of Russians stepped through the rubble,

marching over to the Germans. Russ and Józef followed. A gunshot rang out off to the left. Another to the right. The Russians were killing any Germans still alive. One shot to the head. The *coup de grâce*. Russ walked up to one of the Germans lying facedown in front of the burning Panzer and launched a vicious kick to his side. The soldier didn't move, but Russ kicked another three times, each time imagining the face of Kommandant Strauss, Kapo Burchard, and all the other Nazi sons of bitches that had caused so much death and misery—not only to him, but to his people, and to all of Europe. Russ moved on to several more bodies and repeated the move.

While he and the front line moved forward, the Soviet rear guard swept the remaining houses in the village, kicking down doors, smashing windows, and scouring Torgau for any hidden German soldiers or even sympathizers. Russ shook his head again. Just a few weeks before, *he'd* been the one to be hunted. The tide had turned. From inside one of the houses a hundred meters back, a woman's scream flew through the debris- and body-littered streets. It was a scream of pure terror—one that was answered by the muffled shouts in Russian of several men. Russ paused and looked back. Mikhail, this unit's commander, glared at the American with a look that told him to clear the battlefield and keep moving forward. *Don't ask questions,* he seemed to say with his eyes. *It's not your place.*

Russ moved ahead with the Soviet soldiers. The crackling of a radio popped over the screaming.

"*Allo?*" The unit's radio controller stopped and lifted the radio receiver from his backpack and listened. Lightning-quick Russian spat from the handset, and the controller furrowed his brow. The other soldiers within earshot stopped as well and turned their heads, watching and listening.

"What's he saying?" Russ asked Józef, who stood five meters to his left.

"Shhhh!" the Pole snapped, intent on what was

being said. Even though he spoke Russian, he still had to concentrate, or meaning would escape him.

But then, as if following a cue, the entire group of men, including Józef, shouted as one, raising their arms above their heads and rushing to embrace each other. Russian sentences flew about in ecstatic volleys. The men all spoke over each other. Some wiped tears from their faces. Some came over and cuffed Russ on the shoulders, rattling on at him as if he were some long-lost comrade. The word "*Amerkanski, Amerikanski*" peppered their exclamations. A crowd quickly gathered around him. Russ screwed up his eyes and looked around the crowd of jubilant Soviets. Józef was pushing through the throng toward Russ.

"Did you hear?" the Pole asked, his eyes moist and shining from excitement.

"What is it? What happened?"

"Hitler's dead! Shot himself in Berlin! The Germans have surrendered and the American First Army is just fifteen kilometers that way!" he pointed in the direction of their advance. "The war is over! OVER! We shall all go home!"

Before Józef had finished speaking, the tears ran down Russ's cheeks. He collapsed to the snow-covered ground, weeping like an inconsolable child, his body jerking from the effort. In one instant, all of the pain, suffering, and sorrow of the past years surged through him: crashing in Poland behind enemy lines, joining the Polish Underground, longing to see his wife Penny, only to betray her, attempting to assassinate Kommandant Strauss, getting shot, dying in the hell of KL Himmelweg, planning escape, stealing the weapons, fighting back, fleeing, hiding, and now fighting alongside the Red Army. And now it was all over. His body seemed to melt along with the winter frost. A frost that, once gone, made way for new spring flowers. New life. New beauty.

Leaning over, Józef hooked his arm underneath Russ's and pulled his friend up. While the Russians shouted and danced around them, the two men looked deeply into each other's eyes—without talking, they told each other everything. Everything that they had felt and suffered together after their painful journey.

"Thank you," Russ muttered between sobs.

The Pole nodded. Smiled. Shook his head.

"No," he said, taking Russ by the shoulders. "Thank you."

They reached the bridge that evening. After checking all of the German bodies and tanks, the Red Army pushed forward. Only a few kilometers left. Just outside of the village, the River Elbe opened up and formed a natural boundary between the village and the countryside. It was not as wide as the Bug River back in Poland. A lone bridge stretched over its expanse linking the town to the road beyond.

Russ saw them before he heard them.

On the other side of the Elbe, masses of olive-green

tanks, jeeps, and military trucks lumbered forward in formation. Hundreds of infantry spanned the distance between the vehicles, each carrying an M-1 rifle and some, flamethrowers. Each vehicle bore a familiar red, white, and blue insignia.

The Americans.

"Look," someone said in broken English behind Russ. He stopped marching and turned around. It was Mikhail. He was holding a pair of binoculars out. Russ nodded, took the binoculars and raised them to his eyes. Scanning the mass of troops, he focused on the patches on their left shoulders. A fat black *A* over a red-and-white background.

"American First Army," he muttered, lowering the eyeglasses. Mikhail tapped him on the shoulder.

"You. *Amerikanski*. Go." He smiled and nodded toward the bridge. A surge of emotion welled up inside of Russ. He looked back and forth between the First Army Division and the Red Army platoon. He hesitated, his mind swirling. He looked down at the Red Army uniform he was wearing. He wrung his hands in anticipation.

"Go," Mikhail repeated.

Russ nodded, handed back the binoculars, and turned his back on the Soviets. He took a step forward, stopped, and turned back to Mikhail. He walked up to the Soviet officer and handed him his rifle.

"*Spaseba*," Mikhail said in Russian. *Thank you.*

Russ smiled and stepped onto the bridge.

On the far side of the Elbe, the Americans paused. One lone soldier walked out to meet Russ. A sergeant. The footsteps slapped softly on the stone as each man eased forward, his eyes riveted on the other. *Step, step, step, step.* On either side of the Elbe, the two armies seemed frozen, as if the only people who existed in this war-torn landscape were these two men. Two armies—two nations—meeting together, united by their common hatred of Hitler and everything that he'd represented.

A soft breeze blew across the bridge, chilling

Russ's face, which had burned during the firefight. He paused. He stopped. The American sergeant stopped, eyeing Russ carefully, warily.

And then, as he had done hundreds, thousands of times before, during his basic training, service, and tour in Europe, Russ snapped his heels together, toes apart forty-five degrees, knees unlocked, back straight, chest out. He straightened his left arm along the line where the crease in his pants would be and brought his right hand up to his forehead. In salute.

"Sir," Russ said in the clearest voice he'd mustered since the beginning of the war. "Russ Schueler, United States Air Force, downed on recon and directly supporting friendly forces. Reporting for duty, sir."

The sergeant's eyes widened in disbelief. He glanced over Russ's shoulder at the gathered Red Army platoon. He snapped back to attention and looked Russ in the eye. His eyes glowed with confusion tempered by a hint of relief.

"Soldier?" he mumbled. "Why are you dressed this way? As a Russian?" His hand twitched at his side as if he were unsure whether or not to salute or draw his pistol. Russ hesitated, his jaw working up the strength to talk. "You may speak freely."

Russ relaxed his shoulders and looked the sergeant in the eye. A tear ran over his cheek.

"Yes, sir. It's a long story, but I'm ready to tell it."

GLOSSARY
OF GERMAN TERMS

Aktion: The mass murder of the Polish Jewish elite by Germans. These occurred largely before the implementation of the death camps. Aktionen often consisted of mass roundups and executions.

Appellplatz: Roll call square (in concentration camps).

Einsatzgruppen: Groups of S.S. murderers responsible for the Aktionen.

Ersatz: Replacement. During the war, many everyday items were difficult or impossible to obtain. Ersatz products were cheap substitutes, such as margarine for butter, ground rutabaga for coffee, and saccharine for sugar.

Frakturschrift: German Gothic script.

Judenrein: "Free of Jews." The Nazis would try to render villages and regions "Judenrein" as they implemented their genocide of Europe's Jewry.

Konzentrationslager: Concentration camp.

Krematorium: Crematorium.

Sonderkommando: "Special command." Groups of prisoners tasked with staffing the gas chambers and crematoria in the Nazi death camps.

ACKNOWLEDGEMENTS

THROUGHOUT THE WRITING AND REVISION OF THIS SERIES, Brett Hodus has been invaluable in his editorial and moral support. His expert insights into story and character have been instrumental in taking this series from concept to reality. I cannot thank him enough. I would also like to thank Melanie Austin and Nikki Ramsay for their keen editorial eyes in bringing even more authenticity and precision to these six novels. Finally, I would like to thank Bill Horton, who so many years ago first taught me about the terrible history of the Holocaust. It was he who planted the seed in my mind to pursue this topic, learn as much as I could about it, and now, in turn, educate others so that the memory of those who lost so much can survive. Thank you.